June

To Miss Williams

from Mr Friege

DR ORWELL and MR BLAIR

BY THE SAME AUTHOR

Fiction

At Fever Pitch
Comrade Jacob
The Decline of the West
The Occupation
The K-Factor
Veronica or The Two Nations
The Women's Hour

Non-fiction

Communism and the French Intellectuals
The Left in Europe since 1789
Frantz Fanon
The Illusion: an Essay on Politics, Theatre and the Novel
Cuba, Yes?
The Great Fear: The Anti-Communist Purge under Truman and Eisenhower
Under the Skin: The Death of White Rhodesia
The Espionage of the Saints
Sixty-Eight: The Year of the Barricades
The Fellow-Travellers: Intellectual Friends of Communism
Joseph Losey: A Revenge on Life

DR ORWELL

and

MR BLAIR

A NOVEL

David Caute

WEIDENFELD & NICOLSON
London

The author is grateful to George Orwell's Literary Executor, Mark Hamilton, for kindly granting permission to use the direct and adapted quotations from Orwell's work which are to be found in this fictional narrative.

First published in Great Britain in 1994 by
Weidenfeld & Nicolson

The Orion Publishing Group Ltd
Orion House,
5 Upper Saint Martin's Lane,
London, WC2H 9EA

A catalogue reference is available from the British Library

ISBN 0 297 81438 9

Filmset by Selwood Systems, Midsomer Norton
Printed in Great Britain by Butler & Tanner Ltd, Frome and London

For Anne and Oliver Walston

PROLOGUE

'On my return from Spain I thought of exposing the Soviet myth in a story that could be easily understood by almost anyone and which could be easily translated into other languages. However the actual details of the story did not come to me for some time until one day (I was then living in a small village) I saw a little boy, perhaps ten years old, driving a huge cart-horse along a narrow path, whipping it whenever it tried to turn. It struck me that if only animals became aware of their strength we should have no power over them, and that men exploit animals in much the same way as the rich exploit the proletariat. I proceed to analyse Marx's theory from the animals' point of view...'

[George Orwell, Preface to the Ukrainian edition of *Animal Farm,* March 1947]

CHAPTER I

I don't deny that things had, of late, been difficult on the farm. I never tried to pretend to Mr Blair that it had been a bed of roses. There were the foxes. There was the lawsuit with Mr Frederick, of Pinchfield Farm, which hadn't gone well and which my mum thought my dad should never have got into. And she'd begun to say so, mainly because she was furious about our resident Land Girl, Ellen. My mum and dad were barely talking because of Ellen. You could see it in their faces; my ears were red from slaps – a slap for the lawsuit, a slap for the foxes, a slap for Ellen. But none of this justified Mr Blair telling a whole pack of lies about my dad.

His name was Ronald Jones but he was known to everyone around Porterstone as Ron. He had a lot of friends in the pub. I may have told Mr Blair that my dad had recently been drowning his sorrows – but he was never '*drunk*', and as for him '*lurching*' across the yard, he walked as straight on five pints as on none. Yet what did I read, almost two years later, that in August 1945? This:

Mr Jones, of the Manor Farm, had locked the hen-houses for the night, but was too drunk to remember to shut the pop-holes.

It's true that foxes had struck at our Black Minorca pullets, but there's nothing to prove that my dad had been at fault – I remember him biting his briar pipe and repeatedly hitching his trousers as he surveyed the carnage. You could set traps and poisoned bait but a fox is a cunning brute. Mr Blair simply made it up – '*too drunk to shut the pop-holes*'. And there it was, on the very first page, my dad lurching across the yard then drawing himself a last glass of beer from the barrel in the scullery. But what I'd told Mr Blair was this:

On that particular night I was lying awake wondering what was going to happen to us because of Ellen. When my dad came up to bed after securing the hen-houses his footfall on the stairs was weary but quite steady. Nor was my mum '*already snoring*' (as Mr Blair kindly told the world). I never heard her snore and my room was right next to theirs. What I heard was the familiar thump, thump of my dad's boots on the floor, then some low mutterings, getting louder, then my mum's voice raised:

'Shameless bastard!'

And then (it must have been) a blow, followed by silence, apart from my mum's steady weeping. After that the farm was quiet all night, nothing unusual, but what do we read?

As soon as the light went out there was a stirring and a fluttering all through the farm buildings. Another of Mr Blair's inventions.

Ellen was sent packing the next day. She left a little pink note under my pillow – I still have it. 'Dearest Alex, sorry not to be able to say goodbye. Good luck in everything you do. Please remember me fondly, as I will you. Love, Ellen.' My mum was pale, tight-lipped, and I noticed that her hand shook as she poured the tea. Her eye was purple and swollen. As for my dad, I heard him once or twice, crashing about, and I kept out of his sight. Two days later they took him away. I was in school when it happened. When I came home my mum cut me a sandwich.

'He's gone,' she said. 'They took him.'

I nodded and continued eating. She sat down opposite me, which was unusual, because she liked to be on her feet, sighing, her work never done.

'I had to pay off Jack,' she said. 'There's no money, just debts.'

Jack was my dad's only able-bodied hired hand, unless you counted old Ted Hare, who was 'retired' and willing to put in an hour or two most days for a few bob, unless his asthma got him, or his 'rooms' were bad – rheumatism, it must have been.

'What about Ted?' I asked.

'Ted's willing.'

'But Ted can't – '

'I know what Ted can and can't without any advice from you.'

'When will dad come back?'

She stood up and turned away and busied herself.

'Where's dad gone?' I asked.

'Eat your tea. I'm taking a job in the village.'

'What job?' (I instantly felt it was a disgrace to have a mother with a job – though Ellen had a job, I suppose, but she was young.)

'I'm helping with dinners in the school.'

That flattened me. She had to choose the school, of all places! I could just see the grins across the ugly mugs of Joe Pilkington and Tom Frederick, to name only my worst enemies.

'And I'm helping Mrs Pyke in the shop,' she added. 'Now that her boy's been called up.'

'You'll be serving Mrs Pilkington,' I said.

'You shut your mouth or you'll get one!'

I shut my mouth round a jam roll.

'We'll be living over the shop,' my mum said.

This took a moment to sink in.

'But we live here!'

'We did. Thank your father.'

'What about the farm?'

'Ted will keep an eye.'

'But he's useless!'

'You shut up, hear! I can't be working in the school and in the shop and traipsing out here every night.'

After a while I said: 'I'll stay here, then.'

'You'll do what you're told! Debts, debts, debts! That no-good drunk. I don't suppose you know what a debt is.'

'Yes I do. It's when you owe money.'

'And can't pay.'

Old Ma Pyke rented us a single room with a gas ring over the shop in Porterstone. It was damp and dark and there was only one bed. When you plugged in the electric fire it sparked. We took a suitcase each. My mum was crying all the time. I didn't know how to comfort her and didn't try. I hated that room. After a couple of nights on the sofa, and yelling and rows, and Ma Pyke banging on our door, I skipped school and cycled back to the farm. I found old Ted Hare 'keeping an eye' (he said) and smacking his toothless gums together and sighing. I set about feeding the animals.

My mum didn't come after me. She could no longer bear the sight of the farm.

Mr Blair later came to know all this perfectly well, because I told him (though I may not always have told him the same thing, particularly about my dad), but he chose to make up a fairy story of his own, which I suppose is what writers do, though I'm not a literary man myself, nothing grander than Porterstone Grammar School (that was later), and no doubt Mr Blair felt himself well justified from all the applause he got, and the money he made. But I always took Mr Blair to be a straight sort of man, which was how he regarded himself, and I felt let down by what he did.

He first turned up a couple of weeks after they took my dad away and soon after my mum went to live in the village. I remember seeing this very tall stranger in a baggy tweed jacket hurdling the five-barred gate; who he was and what he was up to I had no idea. He certainly wasn't a local man, I knew them all.

I was driving our old cart-horse, Boxer, at the time, an enormous fellow nearly eighteen hands high, fetching the last of the seasoned timber from the beech spinney, which had been mainly cleared before I was old enough to remember. Boxer always grew lazy without exercise. I don't deny I gave him a few lashes on his rump because he could be obstinate as well as lazy, but with a hide like his my whipping was little more painful than a fly on your nose. Boxer could be difficult: you always had to look out for those iron-shod hoofs when harnessing him up. He'd never accepted the bit and the reins like Clover and Mollie did, and now, as we came up from the beech spinney, he was getting ideas, you could tell.

Anyway, there was this tall, gaunt character watching me intently, and he looked halfway between a gentleman and a tramp. As soon as he opened his mouth you could tell he was a gentleman, definitely not one of us – but a gentleman who wanted to hide the fact.

'It's lucky,' he said, 'that animals don't know their own strength.'

'What, sir?'

'Lucky for us humans.'

It was an odd thing to hear.

'This one's getting ideas, sir,' I said, giving Boxer another lash.

'What's his name?'

'Boxer, sir.'

'That's a good name.'

The stranger then chose to walk along beside me and I noticed the size of his boots, the largest I'd ever seen. It was a mild enough autumn day but he wore a long khaki scarf wrapped round his neck right up to his ears. He had a loose, easy stride and an occasional slow, reluctant, smile which was friendly enough but seemed to belong somewhere else.

He asked me all manner of questions about the local countryside. He wanted to know whether the pond and stream were good for coarse fishing and whether the stream had a name. I said not that I knew of.

'What about the Irrawaddy?' he said, his voice curiously flat and wheezy.

'What's that, sir?'

He kind of hummed a bit:

'On the road to Mandalay
Where the old flotilla lay …'

He wheezed from the effort of humming. 'The delta of the Irrawaddy turns the sea brown with mud,' he added. 'Not a welcoming sight as you arrive by sea.'

We walked on in silence. Then he asked why no other human being was to be seen on the farm. I was in no hurry to talk about that.

'You might find plovers' nests up there,' I said, pointing to the knoll in the long pasture.

'Plovers go for recently ploughed land, not grass,' he said.

When we reached the yard he inspected the hen-house as if he had every right to poke his nose anywhere, and began talking to our two goats as if he'd known them all his life.

'I hope you milk them at first light,' he said. He glanced in on the pigs with special interest and said something about the big bacon manufacturers, I don't know what he said. He seemed more interested in the big boars, and the first thing he asked was their names.

'That one's old Major, our prize Middle White,' I told him.

'And this nasty-looking character?'

'That's Napoleon. He's our only Berkshire. He's no trouble but don't turn your back on him,' I said.

'And this restless, pushy, wild-eyed fellow?'

'That's Snowman,' I said. 'He's lively.'

'He likes an audience. Let's call him Snowball. Snowmen don't move, snowballs gather pace.'

Once Mr Blair had re-named an animal there was no turning back (though he only once did it with a dog, since dogs respond to their names).

'And who's this nimble, shifty little chap?' he asked.

'Squealer. He's a porker.'

'Squealer will do,' he nodded, as if he owned the place.

'He gets ideas, sir,' I said.

'Ideas are in short supply in the English countryside.'

I didn't follow that one. On my parents' tongues 'getting ideas' was the great sin both for men and animals. My dad would even accuse a difficult ewe during the lambing season of getting ideas. A dog who went for the ducks, or bolted off to play retriever before my dad had shot any of the wood pigeons, they were all getting ideas. Every whack I got was for ideas. My mum used to say that Mrs Pilkington, of Foxwood Farm, had ideas above her station.

My mum loathed the Pilkingtons, whereas it was the Fredericks that my dad couldn't stand.

The farmhouse door was closed and I saw the man's eye go up to the chimney. I wasn't going to ask him in for a cup of tea, as my mum might have done, in fact I was quite scared by now. Then he sat himself on the back of the cart, his long legs reaching to the ground, and rolled himself a cigarette from a packet of black shag. I noticed that his lighter hung from a rope attached to his belt.

'Give me something to do. Show me the ropes,' he said after a few drags on the tobacco. I must have stared at him in astonishment. 'You'll need help with some of the heavy work now that you're running the farm,' he went on.

How did he know that?

'My name's Blair, Eric Blair,' he said reluctantly. 'What's yours?'

'Alex Jones, sir.'

He seemed to be weighing my name, as if that, too, was up for grabs, but in the end he just cut me out of the story altogether – me, Joe and Tom, who hung about on the farm after school. He cut us out because we knew too much. But I'm running ahead of myself.

'Aged ten, are you?'

'Twelve, sir.'

He gave me a look: in his estimation I remained ten (though not at all small for my age). He took off his scarf and baggy tweed jacket and helped me unload the beech wood into the barn. That was when I noticed the size of his ears, the deep lines burrowing into his gaunt cheeks – and the scar on his throat. Then he insisted on mucking out the stables, but not five minutes into it he suddenly looked very pale and drawn, his face sort of hollowed out, and he sat down and began coughing and holding his chest. Finally he took out a small packet of tea from his jacket pocket and gave it into my hand.

'I expect you can boil a kettle, Alex.' Abruptly his voice changed into that of a tramp: 'A cup of tea, guv'nor!'

So I brought him into our farmhouse after all. I introduced him to our half-tame raven, Inky, who was looking sorry for himself because my mum always made a fuss of him.

'Let's call him Moses,' Mr Blair said.

The creatures without names, like the sheep, all they did in his famous fairy story was bleat in chorus and behave stupidly.

Mr Blair began coming back to the farm. He never said why and I never asked. He had a thin, haggard face ravaged by lines so deep you could only imagine he'd had a terrible life – and a small moustache. His eyes were very blue and deep-set, as if they were masking their quick movements. He told me he took the train to Porterstone, travelling in a third-class smoker and changing once. He said he always meant to read on the train but could never help staring at the mean wilderness of suburban London opening out into narrow, sooty fields dotted with adverts for Carter's Little Liver Pills. Then it was straggling villages with fake-Tudor villas standing sniffishly apart:

'Laurel shrubberies, golf, whisky, ouija-boards and Aberdeen terriers called Jock,' he said.

There was always a fag-end in his mouth, which I somehow didn't feel went with a gentleman, but I was always pleased to see him though I didn't let on, just as I pretended to be more pissed-off than I was when Joe Pilkington and Tom Frederick showed up at Manor Farm after school. I'd always give them my best greeting:

'So what do *you* want, scumbum?'

This was the routine signal for violence of the twelve-year-old variety, accompanied by soundtracks from American Westerns. Joe Pilkington regularly cycled back to Foxwood Farm in tears over a torn shirt or something, exciting wails from his mum, who had pretensions, whereas Tom Frederick was happy enough with the black eyes he carried back to Pinchfield Farm, where his dad regularly took a strap to him for this or that – Tom's hide was as thick as his head. I never doubted that Joe and Tom showed up at the farm because they were now spying for their dads, who wanted to get their hands on our farm cheap. It wasn't long before they were telling tall stories to their parents about this tall stranger, this 'Mr Blair', who could be anybody or a foreign spy. I could tell what their parents were saying because Joe and Tom each sidled up, separately, when the other wasn't looking, to ask me, in their best bum-suck manner, whether Mr Blair was planning to buy the farm from us. When I passed this on to him – I wasn't sure myself – he just smiled faintly.

'That would depend on the swindlers,' he said.

'Who, sir?'

But he didn't explain. Mr Blair told me things he never let on to Joe and Tom, for example that he didn't like his own Christian name which reminded him of a Victorian book he hated, *Eric, or Little By Little.* Joe and Tom never understood Mr Blair the way I did. They'd make a great show of chortling when he came out with one of his baffling pronouncements: 'So long as I remain alive and well I shall continue to love the surface of the earth, and take pleasure in solid objects and scraps of useless information.' He said it so simply that you couldn't laugh, unless your name was Pilkington or Frederick.

He was a compulsive story-teller and most of it was obviously lies. We weren't fooled but we always wanted more, you couldn't help listening. He told us he'd once been 'down and out' in Paris: 'You have talked so often of going to the dogs,' he said, 'and here at last are the dogs.' At first we thought that 'you' meant us but it meant Mr Blair talking to himself. He played twists and turns like that. I remember one story:

'One night, in the small hours, a murder took place right beneath my hotel window. I was woken by a fearful commotion. A man was lying flat on the stones below. I could just see three figures flitting away and out of sight. Some of us went down. The man's skull had been split wide open with an iron bar.' Mr Blair paused. 'I was back in bed and asleep within three minutes.'

'What happened to the man's body?' I asked.

'How come the police didn't ask you about the three men you'd seen running away?' Joe asked.

'Yeah . . .' Tom said suspiciously.

Tom was soon claiming to have spotted that Mr Blair's stories 'didn't add up' and reckoned he was some kind of Bolshie spy who should be turned in. This was after Mr Blair told us about a French Communist he'd known – his name sounded like Furious. Mr Blair said Furious was a Communist when sober and a patriot when drunk. After four or five pints of wine (Mr Blair must have said litres) Furious would be challenging all foreigners to a fight. Then his friends held him down on the floor of the bar and shouted the French for 'Long live Germany!' and 'Down with France!' ('ar bar lar Frawnce' it sounded). Then Furious always turned purple with rage and puked up over everything. They carried him up to bed like a sack and in the morning he was quiet and polite and reading a Communist paper called Loomanitay.

Tom Frederick put it around that this Bolshie spy who called himself Blair (but Tom wasn't fooled by a false name) had stood there in the barnyard shouting 'Long live Germany!' Tom and Joe also reported to their parents that this Mr Blair had organised us into a 'Home Guard' in case German parachutists fell out of the sky into the pigsties.

Then there was the business of the toads, which Joe said proved that Mr Blair was a 'loony'. Mr Blair spent a lot of time looking for toads in the long pasture down by the pond. He had one in his big hand when he suddenly said:

'How many times have I watched toads mating, and thought of all the important people who would stop me if they could.'

I was sure I understood what he meant, but Joe asked him outright why anyone should stop him. Mr Blair just gave him a look and Joe turned beetroot. I think we were all a bit fed up with Mr Blair's always pointing into the distance – some bird or tree – and saying that young people never looked at anything more than a yard from their noses. You had to follow him on these rambles of his, searching for sloes, hazelnuts and blackberries. 'The best hazelnuts are always out of reach,' he said, reaching up with his long arms. He said hips had a nice sharp taste if you cleaned the hairs off them. Sorrel was good with bread and butter – 'Even marge,' he said scornfully – and so on it went. All quite loony.

Mr Blair also had a particular fondness for the goats, feeding them a special mash from a tin plate, but there you go again, there was always some foreign kind of remark which sent Joe and Tom into rude guffaws, like 'Goats were born free but are everywhere in chains.' Occasionally Mr Blair would offer me a wry smile across his thin moustache. 'It's a kind of quotation,' he'd say to me, ignoring Joe and Tom.

We used to go up to the farmhouse for tea. With Mr Blair's second or third visit this became part of the occasion. He brought cakes and biscuits in his old khaki canvas haversack. I noticed that he took the opportunity to examine the whole house, even my parents' bedroom, which I felt was taking advantage. He prodded the feather mattresses, studied the looking-glasses, tested the horsehair sofa, told me that the Wilton carpet was Brussels carpet, and invented a lithograph of Queen Victoria over the sitting-room mantelpiece (he called it the drawing-room). I now know that in Mr Blair's family the ladies were accustomed to retire after dinner to the 'withdrawing' room, which was fair nonsense as far as my people were concerned. According to my mum, Mrs Pilkington used to lead her lady guests out of her dining-room at Foxwood, leaving the gents to their smoking – though of course my parents had never been invited to Foxwood, we weren't good enough.

Mr Blair was always asking questions. He asked me why we didn't have an aspidistra in the house. He said there would be no revolution in England so long as there were aspidistras in the windows. Tom and Joe made a show of burying their faces in their grubby hands. Mr Blair then asked us rather sternly about our elementary school in the village, what we learned. I could tell he thought we were badly educated. He said he thought it was 'democratic' for everyone to go to the same schools – 'or at least to start off there.' He said we were lucky never to have been buckled into an Eton collar sawing our necks.

I didn't mention to Mr Blair that my dad had wanted to send me to Porterstone Grammar School, but when I took the exam, the 'eleven-plus', I didn't get a scholarship place because my English let me down, though my maths was OK, and my dad couldn't afford the fees. Tom was so thick they wouldn't even let him take the exam, so we were both stuck at the elementary school and likely to be out and driving our Daimlers and 1½-litre Riley Lynx sports tourers when we were fourteen. (My dad said that if I'd spent more time on reading and writing, and less on my car mags, I might have got the scholarship to the grammar school. So he confiscated the mags, but he didn't find them all, and the newsagent in Porterstone used to give me tatty old numbers in return for me doing his newspaper round Sundays.) As for Joe, he'd flunked the eleven-plus and now his shocked parents were sending him to a 'crammer' in Feltenham Saturdays and talking of some swank 'prep' school, though I don't think they could find one which would have him, worse luck.

Joe now announced that his father had put his name down for a school called Ardingly. Mr Blair took no notice of that. He asked us whether our school teachers sent us out looking for caterpillars – Joe and Tom started sniggering. Even I had to join in: caterpillars! You might as well take a bunch of town kids out of school to collect empty bottles. But Mr Blair would go off hunting for caterpillars, 'the silky green and purple puss-moth, the ghostly green poplar-hawk, the privet-hawk, large as one's third finger.' He'd take us down to the pond with nets, dredging away for 'enormous newts with orange-coloured bellies', and so on, but evidently our pond was no good, the ducks had scooped the newts.

He seemed to notice everything in the countryside and had a mania for knowing its name. Anything he saw which he couldn't put the right name to upset him. It was the same with the farm animals, this breed, that breed, as if he was getting on top of things by naming them. Five kinds of caterpillar and so on. His eyes were brilliant and he could name a bird, or shoot it, from a very long way off.

'Where does your father keep his gun oil?' he asked me.

'I don't know, sir.'

'Only Roman Catholics don't oil their guns,' he grumbled.

He was always probing about my family but never when Joe and Tom could listen in with their big ears.

'No brothers or sisters?'

'Not since my mum couldn't have the baby.'

'You're fortunate,' he said. 'Sisters only make you feel guilty.'

'Why, sir?'

'Because of the sacrifices they have to make to see you properly set up in life. They're always going short and never saying anything about it.'

I thought about this: it didn't sound so terrible.

'So when will your father be coming back?' he asked.

'I don't know, sir. Quite soon, I expect.'

He'd give me his look and then set about searching the kitchen for bugs and crunching them underfoot. He had a thing about bugs. As gentlemen go, he was certainly odd. But I always respected him. He wasn't one of us, not our kind, but he was never happy with the order of society. I didn't let on, but I was as surprised as posh Joe Pilkington to watch Mr Blair pour his tea into his saucer and slurp it down with loud sucking noises. My mum had always taught me to eat quietly. Even Mr Blair's way of speaking would change slightly. Spotting an empty bag of my dad's Compass potash, he came up with 'I would'n 'ave nuddin to do wiv chemical fertilisers' – though at other times he scoffed at what he called 'Sunday School' farming.

Sometimes he brought his fishing tackle. He said he'd been passing through the 'grim suburbs' on the train down from London and dreaming of a pool with newts and carp, him sitting on the bank, 'happy as a tinker', with the flies buzzing and the smell of wild peppermint, watching the red float on the green water, and out in the middle of the pool you could see the big fish lying just under the surface, sunning themselves. He always talked like that, as if not catching anything was just as good as landing one. Joe and Tom would boast about the huge carp they'd caught and Mr Blair would give that dry, wheezing chuckle of his: 'A fish you catch gets bigger in the telling,' he said, leaving Joe and Tom to sort that one out across their ugly mugs. He preferred a split-cane rod to a green-heart. He knew all about hooks and gut and catching big carp with No. 5 roach-hooks, but he never caught anything. He said that when he was a lad every mill-stream, moat and cow-pond had fish but now they were either drained or poisoned with chemicals from factories or full of rusty tins and motor-bike tyres.

One day we were fishing in the 'Irrawaddy' but having little luck, when Mr Blair stood up, stretched his long arms, and said: 'We want eight and we won't wait.' He studied us intently. 'Eight what?' he asked.

None of us had a clue.

'Eight Dreadnoughts,' he said. Then he turned to me – he usually turned to me first, which was why Tom accused me of bum-sucking. 'What was a Dreadnought, Alex?'

'Dunno, sir.'

That sort of smile leaked through his gaunt face. 'You're not a pacifist, are you?'

'No, sir!'

'Dread ... nought. Fear ... nothing. They were British battleships. When I was seven I was a member of the Navy League and wore a sailor suit with "HMS *Invincible*" on my cap.'

'When was that?' Joe asked cheekily. 'Before or after the English Civil War?' (Mr Blair always insisted that we call it the English Revolution, but it didn't sound right and none of us knew what he meant when he called himself 'a Cromwellian with the soul of a Cavalier', or some such.)

Just for a moment I thought Mr Blair was about to grab a tuft of Joe's fancy hair, which his adoring mother washed twice a week, but Mr Blair only rolled one of his cigarettes and told us about his own school days. We always listened to every word he said, whether we believed it or not, because we'd never met anyone like him. He had a way of watching you, waiting to see whether you were taken in. Anyway, he was pretty fanciful about his school days:

'At eight years old you were suddenly taken out of your warm nest,' he told us, 'and flung into a world of force and fraud and secrecy, like a goldfish into a tank full of pike.'

Mr Blair told us he'd won some kind of 'secret scholarship' to this posh prep school and how they made him feel humble about it.

'Soon after I arrived I began wetting my bed.'

'How old were you, sir?'

'Eight. I was summoned for a beating. When I shuffled in the headmaster's wife was telling a smart lady with a riding whip that I had to be beaten for wetting my bed. I thought it was the smart lady who was going to flog me and I almost swooned with shame.'

I thought about this: only girls 'swooned'. Then I fell to imagining the lady with the riding whip. I remember this because I had to stay sitting down until I could decently stand up, so to speak.

He told us that the millionaires' sons were given sixpence a week pocket money but he only got twopence. His parents sent the proper money to the school but the Head and his wife sort of kept it from him, though they didn't exactly steal it. (I reckoned they did.) He'd hated the rich kids who were always talking about 'ripping and topping and heavenly' while scoffing down strawberry ices and chocolates on green lawns. And he was never allowed a birthday cake at school because he was poorer than the others. And the porridge was always full of lumps, hairs and black things. And the bowls were filthy with old porridge under the rims. And the towels were always damp and smelled of cheese. He was always hungry, he said.

At Eton, he said, he got only bread and butter for tea because he was just a poor 'Colleger' or 'tug'. I had heard of Eton. I'd seen magazine pictures of swells in top hats and tails. Mr Blair didn't look right for Eton. You had to be some real toff to get in, I thought. The idea that they go hungry there struck us as plain loony. He said he'd been 'hopeless' at games and that all of school life was the weak getting it in the neck from the strong, something like that. You could never tell whether he was complaining or boasting about it.

'My mind was permanently lamed by that school,' he said rather proudly, I thought. With Mr Blair it was always a case of 'the worse the better'.

CHAPTER II

The teas with Mr Blair were what I liked best. He'd get a big fire going and he always scalded the teapot before heaping in the leaves and he had Ten Commandments for Making Tea. He arrived with pots of jam but always insisted on spooning it into a jam dish, you weren't allowed to poke your knife into the jar. He brought us a foul salty paste called Gentlemen's Relish for our toast, and once he turned up with some fresh kippers wrapped in the *News Chronicle*. He brought crumpets and scones, sometimes. I remember the flat jar for the Gentlemen's Relish and the words on the label were in Latin, Mr Blair said.

He told us tall stories about his adventures in Burma, Spain and living as some kind of tramp in Paris, none of which I exactly believed though I didn't exactly disbelieve them either. But he never told the same story twice unless we insisted – he could always remember which ones we'd heard already. There was his Russian friend Boris, down on his luck in Paris, but always cheerful, inking his ankles where they showed through his socks. Mr Blair told us about moustaches in Paris hotels: only the cooks are allowed to wear them, never the waiters or the 'plawnjeers' – Mr Blair had been a 'plawnjeer', which was 'the bottom of the pile'. There was this woman cook who'd scream at him non-stop: 'Unspeakable idiot!' (This made us laugh.) 'What have you done with my strainer? Leave those potatoes alone! Fool!' Joe used to ask him to go through this story again and again, partly because we enjoyed the 'Idiot! Fool!' bits, partly because Joe was secretly on the look-out for 'mistakes' – Mr Blair was never allowed to change the words or the order of telling.

Joe and Tom scoffed his crumpets and jam, conveniently forgetting he was a dangerous spy until he'd gone back to London, whereupon they trotted home to Foxwood and Pinchfield, claiming that he'd 'confessed' to being a Spaniard and a Fifth Column. Did I mention Joe's snide sneers about my mum working in the school kitchen? He also informed me, with a great show of concern, his mug stitched into a smirk, that the Head had warned my mum because I was skipping off, and he was threatening me with the inspector or somebody if I didn't mend my ways. I duly punished the messenger for the message and Joe blubbed, which was normal. I did show up at school once or twice, a thrashing each time, and I spent the odd night with my mum in Ma Pyke's smelly attic, mainly for the hot meal. My mum said I was a chip off the old block and I'd be the death of her. I could tell she was really broken up over my dad and Ellen. I once tried putting my hand on hers, for comfort:

'When did you last cut those nails?' she said. 'Look at them! Filthy! *He* never cut his nails neither.'

Ma Pyke always blamed me for my mum's tears. 'You no-good boy!'

But I prefer to remember Mr Blair. None of us boys was sure where Burma was – somewhere near India. Mr Blair had been sent to a place called Mandalay. He said Mandalay was dirty, 'intolerably hot' and had five 'main products': pagodas, pariahs, pigs, priests and prostitutes. I remember having a clear vision of the pigs but everything else was hazy. My mum had called Ellen a 'prostitute', so I had to make do with dirty, hot streets full of pigs and Ellens. As for the 'priests', they were 'boodists':

'There were moments when I wanted to plunge my bayonet into a jeering boodist priest,' Mr Blair told us.

Mr Blair said he let his Burmese servant undress him: 'You wouldn't let a European do it, would you?' (No doubt our brows furrowed on that one.) Whenever he talked about Burma, it was with a kind of hatred, though not exactly. He described prisoners 'squatting in the reeking cages of the lock-ups' and 'the scarred buttocks' of the men who'd been flogged with bamboos. I vaguely imagined it was the 'boodists' who got the bamboo thrashing.

It was during one of these teas that Mr Blair told us how he'd shot an elephant. I'll always remember how he began the story:

'In Burma I was hated by large numbers of people, the only time in my life that I have been important enough to be widely hated.'

Our mouths must have hung open. He'd been a British police officer and the natives had jeered at him whenever they could.

'I was stuck between my hatred of the empire I served and rage against the evil-spirited little beasts who tried to make my job impossible.'

Then he was informed that an elephant had gone 'must' and was ravaging a bazaar. It was his duty to do something about the elephant.

Tom asked what 'must' meant but Mr Blair ignored him and went on with his story:

'I rounded the hut and saw a man's dead body sprawling in the mud. The elephant had ground him into the earth. His face had scored a trench a foot deep and a couple of yards long.'

Mr Blair hadn't wanted to shoot the elephant but didn't dare lose face in front of the natives. He aimed for the swelling in the elephant's forehead, thinking the brain must be there, the result being that the elephant took an hour to die. Then the crowd of natives hacked the great beast to bits, for the meat.

After tea Mr Blair rolled himself another fag, wheezing over the rotten state of the kitchen garden and my mum's flower garden. He said he'd bought a rambler rose which cost him sixpence at Woolworth's. It had grown rapidly and produced a pretty little white rose with a yellow heart. Joe and Tom being out of earshot, I confided to Mr Blair that my mum would no longer come near the farm.

He nodded. 'She's an exile, then.'

'Oh no, sir, she's English.'

He stooped to finger the ravaged cabbages. The rabbits, reassured by the silences round the empty farmhouse, had been getting ideas. Mr Blair sighed over the remains of my mum's lobelias and dahlias.

'It's animal farm now,' he said.

'Sir?'

He took my air gun and potted a couple of rabbits, just like that. Obviously the elephant had never stood a chance. 'He neither stirred nor fell,' Mr Blair had told us, 'but every line of his body had altered.'

What bothered him most, I thought, was that he hadn't

possessed the right knowledge to shoot the elephant properly. He hated not to know how to do things, or how things worked, or why something had happened, and he always insisted on this or that cause, however fanciful. For example, we found one of our ganders dead near the pond and not a mark on him, couldn't have been foxes, so Mr Blair turns detective and spots some deadly nightshade. 'Ergo,' he says and cuts it down. Joe and Tom fairly creased themselves. (And then, two years later, on page 83 of the master work, a gander *commits suicide* by swallowing deadly nightshade. Mr Blair certainly had a queer kind of mind, but it brought him fame and fortune, so there you go.)

Mind you, Mr Blair was always very hot on poisons and bites. He told us that townspeople talked a lot of nonsense about it – they thought that snakes stung, whereas they bit; they thought that lizards, slow-worms, toads, frogs and newts all stung. They thought that raw potatoes were deadly poison.

Tom then declared that some snakes do sting. Mr Blair said that stinging is like throwing a spear – it leaves your hands and lodges in the victim – whereas biting was like using a sword – you hang on to it. Tom looked sullen and Joe shifty – he was hoping I'd made the same mistake.

Later that afternoon Mr Blair sat himself on a tree stump in the long pasture, rolled another fag of Nosegay black shag pipe tobacco in his little machine (his fingertips were stained a deep brown), and told us exactly how much he spent on cigarettes and how much on books, as if his habits were a scandal.

'I've worked it out,' he said. 'I reckon I own about nine hundred books, which I've acquired during the past fifteen years and which probably cost me a hundred and sixty-five pounds fifteen shillings. That works out at eleven pounds one shilling a year, you see. Add to that two daily papers, one evening paper, two Sunday papers, one weekly review and one or two monthly magazines. That brings the figure up to nineteen pounds one shilling, you see. On top of that there are the Penguins and cheap editions one buys and throws away. So let's say I'm in the neighbourhood of twenty-five pounds a year on reading matter. Now we come to my smoking: six ounces a week, at half a crown an ounce, making nearly forty pounds a year, you see. In fact the ordinary Englishman spends more on cigarettes than an Indian peasant has for his whole livelihood.'

He smiled bleakly at us: 'So there you are. Not a proud record for a country which is nearly a hundred per cent literate.'

Then he let out that he'd been a schoolmaster, but not for long. He said private schools were a 'squalid racket' run by 'profiteers' who just wanted to grab the fees. I saw Joe and Tom exchange smirks and I have to admit that he sank even in my estimation: after shooting the man-killer elephant and living as a tramp, it was no great thing to have become a schoolmaster – even if he wasn't one any longer. (Though Joe said he reckoned he was, because of the caterpillars.)

Mr Blair must have sensed that being a schoolmaster had earned him no marks, because he abruptly re-enlisted us in the 'Home Guard' and started talking about making petrol bombs from milk bottles. I think he was half tempted to show us how it was done – you often felt he was being pulled two ways. Tom Frederick, who always claimed not to be 'taken in' and to know for certain that Mr Blair was a spy, now came up with a 'cunning' question intended to 'trap the Bolshie' (as he loudly put it whenever the Bolshie was safely in London).

'Why do you think Adolf would bomb this farm, sir? Have you been a pilot in the Luftwaffe, sir?'

Mr Blair promptly produced from his haversack a pile of old boys' weeklies, mainly *Magnet* and *Gem.*

'These are standard issue to all Luftwaffe pilots,' he told Tom, then keenly watched the three of us scuffling over the adventures of Billy Bunter, Harry Wharton & Co. Any minute and he might be on again about Rudyard Kipling, the jungle writer.

'I worshipped Kipling at thirteen,' Mr Blair had once confided to me (and me alone) when he and I were fishing for carp (he was a wizard with worms). 'At seventeen I loathed Kipling, at twenty I enjoyed him, at twenty-five I despised him – and now again I rather admire him.'

I could tell that Mr Blair liked me. I think he rather enjoyed the mists of uncertainty (as he put it) in my eyes because you'd get a sly, searching glance, almost tender – which wasn't the way he looked at Tom and Joe.

As we sat by the pond he touched my shoulder and said: 'Can the carp reason with the heron? Can the worm reason with the carp, Alex?'

He spoke in that rather dry, flat way, his voice strangely weak and reedy, as if his throat had been damaged. Just to listen to him, you would never have guessed what he looked like.

Sometimes on those damp autumn days we'd sit on a log in the meadow, or light a wood fire in the barn (he had some fancy ideas about the barn owls, too), and he'd read us extracts from the Billy Bunter stories. He was always telling me the farm needed work but Tom and Joe preferred stories. I realise now that while the mild weather lasted things didn't seem so bad, there was grass and fodder, and perhaps I still expected my dad to drop out of the sky and put everything to normal. I'm not sure about that. Old Ted Hare was still putting in an hour or two, drinking tea, unless his asthma was playing up or his 'rooms' were bad. As for my mum, she left me in peace, mostly, unless I went near her.

Mr Blair was quite good at reading, quite funny, and he clearly enjoyed himself whenever Harry Wharton & Co. were 'landed and stranded, diddled, dished and done' – as they always were. But then you'd get that sly, searching glance and he wanted to know what we thought about the posh schools these comic kids went to, and I always found myself competing with Tom and Joe to give the clever answers that Mr Blair seemed to be waiting for. If he didn't get them the likely outcome was a strong lecture denouncing comics – how they had 'no political development whatever', how they were all out of date, how there was all this 'leader-worship' in *Wizard* and *Hotspur*, how the Russian Revolution was hardly ever mentioned, and why were there no booms, slumps, unemployment, dictatorship, purges or concentration camps – and why was there no facing of the facts about working-class life?

At this Joe Pilkington went on his dignity and adopted his 'I'll tell my mum' look. Who was Mr Blair calling 'working-class'? Tom just looked stupid and pulled a long strand of snot from his nose.

Did we believe Mr Blair had really been a tramp? I don't know. I think we believed he'd gone hop-picking in Kent because London people did that. He said the hops gave the beer its 'kick' but nowadays the hops all went for chemicals, and the chemicals went into the beer. He said you could always cadge tea from the Kentish housewives if you doffed your cap and said, 'Please, ma'am, could you spare me a pinch of tea?' He talked of sneaking into private woods and 'drumming up', cooking squalid meals in two-pound snuff-tins. Mr Blair claimed to have fallen in with a young thief called Ginger who filched knives and forks from Woolworth's, and cigarettes from a grocer's when 'we were perishing for a smoke'. Mr Blair said that Ginger even wanted to rob a church but Mr Blair had talked him out of it. 'I expected to get pinched,' Mr Blair said, 'but never pulled it off.' Then there was the old man of Kent who used to 'exhibit' himself to women and children – the only way I understood this word was showing your best pigs and cattle at the local fair, so I was baffled by that one and didn't ask.

But tramping in London – I was never sure if it was all made up. He described a 'kip' or 'spike', which cost a shilling a night, and how one old man coughed all through the night, 'a foul bubbling and retching, as though the man's bowels were being churned up within him.' (We all went 'Ugh . . .') The same man wore his filthy trousers round his head as a nightcap, which had disgusted Mr Blair. Then he told us that all the bugs in London lived south of the river because they couldn't swim. (That one deserved a lot of thought.) He could make your flesh creep, though – I won't forget the dry way he described the slums of Lambeth, the narrow, puddled streets plunged in darkness, the few lamps mist-ringed and illuminating nothing but themselves (as he put it). He used to walk under some echoing railway arches and up on to Hungerford Bridge where people were murdered or did themselves in.

But when he talked of the glow of the sky-signs on the water he cheered up because he was quite a nut about adverts. He pretended to despise them but the catch-phrases would slip out for no reason at all, as if they were *djinns* haunting him. (He had a joke from his time in Burma about *djinn* and tonic which I got at once – my mum said Mrs Pilkington was too fond of gin and tonic.) Mr Blair would be sitting by the pond not catching anything when he'd suddenly say, 'Prompt relief for feeble kidneys.' When he took himself to our outside privy he'd smile faintly and say, 'Silkyseam – the smooth-sliding bathroom tissue.' I remember the time Tom was practically accusing him to his face of being a Bolshie German spy when Mr Blair raised his eyebrows and said to Tom: 'Are *you* ashamed of your undies?' He couldn't get on his bike to ride into Porterstone without a 'Hike all day on a slab of Vitamalt!' Later on – I'll come to this presently – when he stayed with me for several days at a very difficult time for me, he emerged from a shave with 'Now I'm schoolgirl complexion all over.'

On one occasion Joe boldly asked Mr Blair what he did for a living, and Tom nodded 'Yeah,' as if this would unmask the spy. Mr Blair said he'd been wasting his time working at the BBC and broadcasting 'imperialist propaganda' to India, but fortunately the Indians weren't listening, and now he was back to writing. Joe got clever and asked why a 'real' writer should always be spouting advertising slogans.

Mr Blair slowly rolled and lighted a fag (he never used a match – matches were dead scarce).

'I suppose,' he said slowly, 'that copywriters are novelists' monkeys. And maybe the other way round, too.'

Well, there was some explosion from all of us – even I couldn't hold it back. It was some years before I realised he must have said 'novelists *manqués*'. Joe later rushed off home to inform his shocked mama that this Mr Blair said that adverts were written by chimpanzees.

So what was he writing? I asked.

'A fairy story which both grown-ups and children might enjoy.'

'What's it about, sir?'

'A farm.'

For us a pot of tea wouldn't have been a duller subject and Joe and Tom immediately went into their routine scoffing and groaning.

'Talking pigs, sir?' Joe asked cheekily.

Mr Blair nodded. 'That sort of thing. They can read and write too.' Then he added: 'It's just an idea. It may not be as good an idea as Billy Bunter or Mowgli.'

This might sound humble but I wouldn't call Mr Blair humble. He always had to be on top of things. At heart he was always your schoolmaster, always stretching our dull minds by way of tests and competitions. But Mr Blair's competitions were a good deal more entertaining than the ones we struggled through in school. One of his favourite games in the farmhouse kitchen during tea was called 'True or False'. He would make a statement and each of us would have to say whether it was true or false. A correct answer scored three points, a wrong answer one, and no answer none. Tom hardly ever risked an answer, Joe always waited to hear mine then studied Mr Blair's expression before making up his mind, but Mr Blair was wise to that and punished Joe's dodges with penalty points which Joe said weren't fair. Mr Blair kept the score on scraps of paper headed with the printed words British Broadcasting Corporation. I can still remember some of his questions:

A swan can break your leg with its wing: true or false?

A boy goes blind if he fiddles with himself: true or false?

All toadstools are poisonous: true or false?

You can be had up for putting a stamp with the King's head upside down on a letter: true or false?

There is a reward of £50 for spending a night in the Chamber of Horrors at Madame Tussaud's: true or false?

Men will land on the moon within thirty years: true or false?

(We never doubted that his answer on that was the last word on the subject, though I can't remember what it was.)

You cannot love a person you fear: true or false?

(This drew no response; 'love' was not a word any of us could utter.)

An elephant's food is bananas: true or false?

Christopher Columbus discovered the USA: true or false?

(Joe argued about this and was punished by the loss of two points. He argued some more about *that*, and lost five points.)

The Left Book Club is books you can buy cheap because they were left in railway carriages: true or false?

Bulls are enraged by the colour red: true or false?

Africans and Orientals are not subject to sunstroke: true or false?

Adolf Hitler has only one ball: true or false?

Light travels slower than sound: true or false?

(When we all got that one wrong Mr Blair advised us to keep our eyes and ears open during the next thunderstorm. Joe, a knowall who regularly fell out of trees, turned red enough to enrage – or not – a bull and declared that the sound of a storm came later because it had further to travel.)

Mr Blair had another game called the 'As Game' – but this was for me alone. I never told Joe or Tom about it. It wasn't competitive and you could take your time. Generally Mr Blair played it when the two of us were fishing for carp in the pond and not catching any.

'As noisy as ... As painful as ... As proud as ...' Of course his own solutions were always the best and I remember a few of them: 'As noisy as a mouse in a packet of macaroni.' And another: 'Boys crammed with learning as cynically as a goose is crammed for Christmas.' (I didn't understand 'cynically'.)

But he could sit around only for so long before hauling himself up and looking for practical things to do. I think he hated idleness. You'd often find him mixing too much of our scarce mash with some swill in the sties and he seemed particularly interested in the oldest boar on the farm, Major, who had once been exhibited by my dad under the name of Porterstone Beauty. Major now spent ninety per cent of his time asleep but Mr Blair used to talk to him as if he was wide awake.

'Never had your tushes cut, hm?'

Mr Blair asked me whether I thought old Major was 'getting ideas'.

'He's no trouble, sir,' I said.

'Maybe he's dreaming something up.'

'Animals don't dream, sir – except perhaps dogs. A dog will dream of stealing biscuits ... sometimes.'

I felt on shaky ground here and Mr Blair was wearing a grim smile. He began to talk to the two boars my dad had been breeding up for sale at fifteen stone, Snowball and Napoleon, who I'd let out into the field with the horses to scavenge for themselves. Napoleon was angrily snuffling around and kicking aside little Squealer.

'Napoleon wants power,' Mr Blair said.

'He's hungry, sir.'

'Hungry for power,' Mr Blair corrected me. He then looked slightly guilty and five minutes later he produced some assorted sweets from a crumpled bag in his pocket, bull's-eyes and pear drops mainly. He never handed them round, he just dropped the bag to observe our behaviour, as if carrying out some kind of laboratory experiment, like they do on animals. Tom's paw was always the first to reach out. Joe and I vied with each other to hold back.

'In my day,' Mr Blair said, 'you could buy Farthing Everlastings, which were a yard long and couldn't be finished inside half an hour. There was an old hag in our village store called Mother Wheeler and we suspected her of sucking the bull's-eyes and putting them back in the bottle ... though it was never proved.'

'Ugh!' Joe groaned obligingly. Tom was frowning, never sure what to believe. I was imagining the slimy-wet bull's-eyes dropping from the old hag's toothless gums back into the jar. I could almost hear her cackle. Mr Blair was watching me.

'When was the last witch burned in England, Alex?'

CHAPTER III

Mr Blair was a nutter for collecting things, stamps, old coins, cigarette cards, birds' eggs, picture-postcards showing ladies with big bums in swimsuits. He always let us keep any we wanted – his steady eye alert to whether I kept them, Joe kept them, or Tom kept them. I knew he preferred me to have them but he also wanted me not to grab them. If I couldn't control myself because I badly needed some cigarette card for my collection, there'd be a long pause and then something like this:

'To each according to his needs, is that it? What does socialism mean to you, Alex?'

I said socialism was when they took your farm away and everyone stayed in bed all day with bad women.

Mr Blair said socialism was when everyone had a hot bath every day. That sounded even worse but I was pleased he always said these things to me, and never bothered much with Joe or Tom. As I recall, talk of socialism often set him thinking about fishing, and out would come our rods and tackle. I began to associate socialism with digging for worms. He also showed me how to pour turpentine down a wasps' nest and plug up the hole with mud until the wasps were dead and you could dig out the grubs. He said 'grubs' and 'bait' like he said 'workers' – with a kind of solid respect.

'Of course,' he said, 'live grasshoppers are best for chub. You flick them on the surface of the water, it's called "dapping".' So Mr Blair showed me dapping, his big feet deep in mud, quietly cursing our kingfisher who was 'spoiling the patch', but there were no chub, merely drowned grasshoppers. Watching his float lying placidly on the muddy surface of the 'Irrawaddy' set him musing and wheezing:

'You have all those millionaires trout-fishing in private waters round Scotch hotels,' he said. 'It's a sort of snobbish game of catching hand-reared fish with artificial flies.'

I wasn't arguing with that (or anything). Then he said he had a 'literary friend' called Connolly who'd been at school with him and who was very short and fat and drank a lot of champagne and married an American. Then he muttered something about this Connolly and a rock-pool and 'human lizards' but I didn't get it. Then he said that this Connolly said that the gentry and aristocracy showed good sense by catching fish you could eat, whereas the working man was in it just for the hunting while complaining loudly about fox-hunting.

'So I set Connolly straight about that,' Mr Blair said, gazing at his float rather intently. 'I set him straight,' Mr Blair repeated, 'but of course he's perfectly right. But I can't tell him he's perfectly right, can I? He was at school with me, after all. You wouldn't tell Joe or Tom they were right about anything, would you?'

'No, sir!'

'Well, there you are. How can I tell Connolly he's perfectly right? He'd probably demand a bottle of claret, you see, and nothing cheap. So I reminded Connolly that all our fancy fish have French names whereas your roach, rudd, dace, barbel, pike, bream, gudgeon, chub, carp and tench are solid English names.'

We sat in silence. I was trying to imagine the fat lizard, Connolly, who liked wine.

'So guess what Connolly said,' Mr Blair eventually wheezed.

'What, sir?' (By now I was completely absorbed in this contest.)

'Connolly said that everything worthwhile has a French name – liberty, justice, socialism, equality, wine, pleasure – everything except women, love and cheese, he said – whereas I was sitting on the banks of polluted streams trying to catch fish with names as non-French as pail, nail, snail and tail.'

Another silence. I asked Mr Blair whether he'd ever eaten snails and frogs in France.

He nodded. 'Certainly.'

He had quite a mania for the 'Home Guard'. He used to drill the three of us for up to half an hour using carved sticks from the giant sycamore tree as rifles.

'In open country bullets are fairly straightforward,' he told us. 'In towns they have a habit of coming round corners.' We stared at him in disbelief. 'They nearly always ricochet,' he explained. Then he sat down to get his breath and asked us if we'd played with tin soldiers when we were 'kids'. Joe said his soldiers were real lead. Mr Blair nodded bleakly:

'No socialist would be pleased to find his son playing with toy soldiers. Difficult to find a substitute – toy pacifists somehow won't do.'

Then he mentioned that he'd recently seen some mannequins lying on the pavement outside a bombed department store in London. 'They looked like a pile of corpses.'

When we did well in his estimation, and lay on the wet

ground in dead silence for ten minutes, ready to ambush 'the Fascist Fifth Column', we might be rewarded with a tin of bully beef for tea.

'So what's that then, sir?' Tom asked cunningly. 'This Fifth Column of yours?'

'Blackshirts behind the lines,' Mr Blair said.

Now it so happened that Mr Blair himself sometimes wore very dark blue shirts, close to black, so Tom and Joe promptly told their dads that his tall stranger was a Fifth Column. Joe said his mum wanted to know why this able-bodied gent wasn't serving his country like everyone else who wasn't in 'essential war work'. Mr Frederick alerted Constable Gill, who in turn spent hours 'hidden' in the copse waiting for the Bolshie while studying filthy pictures and stories in the *News of the World.* Eventually the constabulary grew bored and accused us boys of 'spreading rumours' – apparently a war crime for which hanging was the 'minimum penalty'.

When Mr Blair next showed up in his baggy tweed jacket, Joe and Tom looked slightly ashamed of themselves. I didn't let on to Mr Blair what they'd done but I did confide to him that Constable Gill had been on the lookout for him.

'So where is he?' Mr Blair asked.

'He got bored waiting around, sir.'

'How can we defend our freedom against spies if our police officers get bored?' Mr Blair said.

'I dunno, sir.'

Mr Blair then explained that he'd often tried to get himself arrested.

'Why, sir?'

'To see what prisons are like from the inside. But even when leading a tramp's life I never pulled it off. It's probably my accent,' he said gloomily, 'the giveaway aitches. In the end I had to settle for second-best, as a prison visitor, which isn't the same thing at all. You walk out scot free, you see.'

In London (he told us) he was presently a Home Guard sergeant with ten men under his command. He said there was too much drilling and that the men were being used as toy soldiers by 'Colonel Blimps'. Mr Blair wanted to 'arm the people'. He wanted us boys to practise 'gorilla warfare' round the farm. He pointed out the part of the long pasture where an enemy plane might attempt to land, and issued elaborate instructions about harnessing Boxer and Clover to the carts to block the 'runway'. But then he thought again and reckoned it would be too late and urged us to dig deep holes all over the 'runway' so that the German plane would crash on landing.

'I think the sheep would fall in and break their legs, sir,' I said.

But there was a kind of fever in him and he strode up to the knoll to inspect the ruined windmill for the umpteenth time, prodding the rough stones with his big boot and muttering to himself about 'sabotage' and 'dynamite', but you couldn't tell how serious he was.

'It blew down in a gale, sir,' I always explained.

'Is that what they told you?'

The way he said 'they' made you glance over your shoulder towards the spinney. But then he asked us where the word 'sabotage' came from and none of us had a clue.

'In northern France *sabot* means a heavy wooden shoe,' he said. 'Working men used to wear them. One day some workers with a grievance against their boss threw their *sabots* into the machinery while it was running.' He looked at us, then smiled faintly: 'True or false?'

Joe and Tom hesitated. 'True,' I said.

But Mr Blair had already lost interest; his gaze was now fixed on the distant flight of my mum's pet raven, who'd gone half-wild from hunger, and who was squawking irritably round the sycamore.

'That's Moses,' Mr Blair said. 'Sugarcandy Mountain beyond the clouds. All animals go there after they die.'

Tom guffawed loutishly while Joe confined himself to his superior smirk. Mr Blair then rolled a fag and asked each of us whether we were church, chapel or 'nothing'. My first thought on this was the memory of my mum and Mrs Pilkington in contention to provide the biggest vegetable marrows to decorate the side altar and font during the Harvest Festival.

'We do up the church during the Harvest Festival,' I said, and Joe chipped in, 'Us too!'

Mr Blair nodded his nod: 'Festoons of runner beans, prize tomatoes, with the marrows a kind of Stonehenge of paganism.' He turned to the silent Tom: 'Dissenter, are you? A Tin Tabber? Turn your prayers into money every day of the week? Congregationalist? Wesleyan? Baptist?'

'Yeah,' Tom mumbled.

'So which of you believes in heaven and hell?' Mr Blair asked.

After some hesitation we all raised our hands.

'Do you believe in hell like you believe in Australia?' Mr Blair pressed. 'Can you get on a boat and be sure of landing there several weeks later?'

Joe said you fly there.

'So why shouldn't the raven Moses fly to his own Sugar-candy Mountain?' Mr Blair asked.

'Because that's daft, sir,' Joe said. 'Birds don't have souls.'

Mr Blair asked us what you have to do to go to hell. Tom said Catholics go to hell.

A few moments later, I don't remember how the conversation turned, Joe was boasting to Mr Blair how his dad had made money buying and selling building plots before the war. This may have had something to do with the Pilkington flight-path to heaven, I'm not sure.

'And you, Joe,' Mr Blair asked, 'will you do the same?'

Joe was obviously flattered to be treated as a future adult and it wouldn't have surprised me if he'd pulled out a packet of Craven A and lighted one there and then. (Mr Blair always said 'lighted', not 'lit'.) Of course all the boys were smoking a bit, for a lark, but you wouldn't dare with Mr Blair around.

'I might well be into that,' Joe announced. 'Building plots is the thing.'

Mr Blair turned to me. 'You'll be a farmer,' he said. 'Make sure you don't sell out your heritage, the good farming land of England, to property developers. Or newspaper proprietors. Or simple-lifers on a thousand pounds a year. Make sure they don't fill in your pools and ponds with concrete. Don't let them desecrate your meadows with those faked-up Tudor houses with curly roofs and buttresses which don't buttress anything. Those rock-gardens with concrete bird-baths and red plaster elves. The Laurels, The Myrtles, The Hawthorns, Mon Abri, Mon Repos, Belle Vue.'

Joe Pilkington had turned beetroot. I happened to have confided to Mr Blair that Joe's mum had persuaded his dad to pull down a large part of their damp old King George farmhouse and put up something fancy and (my mum said) tasteless. She'd called it Belle Vue. Mrs P. was very keen on bird-baths, too.

But my own life during that winter of 1943–4 had nothing to do with curly roofs or bird-baths, and Mr Blair knew it. Our animals were becoming hungrier by the week. Some died. By the time of the January frosts the domestic cats were half-wild and going for the chickens. The dogs were beginning to lose their homing instinct as they hunted further afield for rabbits and hares. The heavier animals like Boxer and Clover and Benjamin the donkey started breaking through thorn hedges which they would never normally have challenged. I spent hours searching them down. The sheep and goats made a pathetic din, crowding round, kicking and butting, whenever I turned up with fodder.

As for Joe and Tom, they never did a hand's turn to help. I knew they only showed up under orders from their dads, each biding his time to buy our farm cheap, waiting for the moment when we could no longer hold out. Our four sows had farrowed in the autumn, producing some thirty piglets; Pilkington and Frederick had already carried some of them off on the cheap because otherwise the hungry sows would have eaten them.

I explained this to Mr Blair but I didn't mention how often I was skipping school, or the Ford car that arrived in the farmyard, a man in a hat looking for me, and how Ted Hare played the village idiot (without effort) and smacked his gums and sighed, no idea where I was, probably with my mum – though Ted knew I was hiding in the barn. It was only a two-door Ford 8, which you could pick up second-hand for fifty quid, like my dad had done before he had to sell it because of the debts; it wasn't even the four-door, 1,172cc Model C Ten that Pilkington flaunted like a Rolls.

I didn't mention to Mr Blair how I'd gone back to Ma Pyke's shop one afternoon to ask my mum what price she got for the piglets, only to be told that 'they' had taken my mum to some hospital, 'because of her nerves', and it was all my fault, you no-good boy, and 'they' were looking for me, to take me 'in'.

'You can't stay here on your own,' Ma Pyke said. As if I wanted to. 'Mrs Pilkington is offering to have you. She was in here only this morning, very concerned for you, she is.'

Just imagine. I lifted some currant buns and a small jar of jam from the shop on my way out. I didn't tell any of this to Mr Blair because you can never quite trust an adult.

He did everything he could to help me keep the big boars and porkers going – but he was always 'talking' to the pigs about 'revolution' and humming a song called 'Beasts of England' which he claimed he'd learned from old Major. I think he made that up because I told him my dad had been planning to send the old boar for slaughter. Mr Blair also claimed that old Major was having 'a long and wonderful dream' and must be allowed to convey it to the other animals before dying. I told Mr Blair he was pulling my leg. He put on his longest face and asked where my leg was hurting.

He had a knack for making you feel guilty. For example in the harness room. He had a special thing about cruelty to animals. He wasn't keen on us shooting at chaffinches with catapults or raiding birds' nests. When a schoolmaster, he'd once thrashed a boy for blowing up a frog with a bicycle pump. He used to hang about my dad's harness room grumbling about the bits, nose-rings, and dog-chains – and also the knives my dad had used to castrate pigs and lambs. I don't know why Mr Blair thought the nosebags for Boxer and Clover were 'degrading'; as for the blinkers, which he also took against, they simply save the beast from fright when it's out on the road. The whips you could argue about – but there again Mr Blair had told us how he regularly used a stick when he was a schoolmaster, so why the fuss? Let a big horse like Boxer get ideas and you'll be sorry.

Then there was our collection of snares – Mr Blair said they were the 'crudest and cruellest' he'd ever seen. He said the test of a good snare was how quickly the animal died. My dad had taught me that the test of a snare is whether you get the bugger or you don't. Mr Blair set about making some fancy snares of his own devising but he never bagged a single rabbit or mole. What he did get was rats, by mistake, because I'd say Mr Blair's whole nature changed when he set eyes on a rat. Even a dead one, he could barely bring himself to pull it from the trap and if we boys hadn't been watching he'd have walked on, searching the sky for plovers' nests and Sugarcandy Mountains. Any of us would cheerfully seize a farm rat by its tail and bang its brains out but Mr Blair confessed he had a phobia, which lodged in my head as 'fobeer'. He told us how when he was in the trenches in Spain he'd shot a rat which was annoying him in his dugout, the result being that firing broke out all along the front, even artillery and machine guns, leaving the cookhouse and two buses destroyed. He told this story with a straight face but we laughed a great deal. He also read aloud a passage from *Gulliver's Travels* where Gulliver, washed ashore in Brobdingnag, is attacked by two giant rats with tails 'two yards long, wanting an inch'. Mr Blair said that was the worst moment in the book for him, though he enjoyed the 'wanting an inch'.

'I estimate I'd betray my country *and* my friends if my captors threatened to let rats loose on me,' Mr Blair told me. But he didn't mention this to Joe and Tom.

One thing I noticed: it was when snares didn't snare or

bonfires didn't light or the effort of digging left Mr Blair pale and exhausted – it was at such times that he was more likely to talk about his work in London. As if, somehow, he was admitting that his real life was there, not here. He told us about the famous people who did the broadcasts for him to India, but we'd never heard of any of them. I remember him telling me he was paid £680 a year by the BBC: 'It's not riches,' he smiled, 'but it's not out-at-elbow either.'

He told us how he wrote a sort of play for radio from a story called *The Fox* by an Italian writer. To do an Italian writer seemed to us as bad as a German writer but Mr Blair said this writer, Silone, was against Mussolini and the Fascists. He said the story began when a farmer was looking after his sow by giving her castor oil to help litter her seven piglets. Joe said the farmer must be a Fascist because Mussolini forced castor oil down the throats of his prisoners.

'But not the throats of his pigs,' Mr Blair said. Anyway this farmer was worried about a fox who'd been getting into the chicken-runs and breaking necks on a big scale. But the main point of the story was that there was also a 'human fox' sneaking about, a spy for the Fascists.

Then Mr Blair asked me whether we were much bothered by foxes here on Manor Farm. I told him that foxes had killed some of our Black Minorca pullets.

'So what did your dad do?' he asked (very intently, I thought, he was seriously interested).

I told him that foxes were dead cunning and avoided every kind of trap and poisoned bait. So it was the gun or nothing. Mr Blair's blue eyes were alight: 'The farmer in Silone's story had the same problem,' he said, fiddling with his tobacco.

Then he said: 'You might have a human fox round here, Alex.'

I stared at him. To this day I'm not sure what he meant but my guess, and it's only a guess, is this: writers are foxes. But what I'm dead sure of is the fox-trail from that Italian story to another story we all now know.

When Mr Blair wasn't about, which was most of the time, Joe and Tom used to swagger around Manor Farm in their warm winter coats scoffing about him. Joe said the man was straight out of a bin and an 'impostor' (clearly a word borrowed from Joe's dad) who knew nothing about farming but liked to talk learnedly about field-drains, silage and basic slag. I said Mr Blair knew quite a bit because he'd warned me to put extra straw on the potato clamp. (Mr Blair said he'd buried large quantities of his own potatoes for long-term storage but when he dug them up they were too mouldy to eat. I remember him telling me this, leaning on a hoe, very frail somehow, and how strong his legs looked in their cord trousers compared to his thin body and hollowed-out chest.)

Joe sneered at Mr Blair behind his back for his crackpot plan for the animals to drop their dung directly in the fields, at a different spot every day, to save the labour of cartage. I knew Joe was right but I wasn't saying so and there were more fights. My nerves were raw, my hands were frozen, I was often hungry and close to exhaustion. In a fight I was now an opponent dangerous beyond my years and strength, and Joe and Tom began to keep their distance. Their sneers came with the wind.

What I didn't know was that Mr Blair's dung-drop scheme would later surface in the mind of our boar, Snowball, with chaotic results. And I may as well add here that Snowball's famous ground plan for a new windmill, complete with dynamo to generate electricity for a circular saw, a chaff-cutter, a mangel-slicer, an electric milking machine and you name it – this scheme was also Mr Blair's. It was he who drew plans in chalk on the smooth wooden floor of the shed which had once been used for incubators. And if you want to know who really pissed over the plans, when Mr Blair was away in London, it certainly wasn't Napoleon. In my mind it was ten to one on Tom Frederick, pissing for his shilling.

Anyway, a clear case of sabotage but nothing to do with French workmen throwing their wooden shoes about.

CHAPTER IV

What I hated was the way Joe and Tom always showed up, all smiles, whenever Mr Blair paid a visit. All smooth and smarmy, particularly Joe. 'We must all do our best to help poor Alex.' They knew I couldn't bloody their noses with Mr Blair around. At the time I felt he didn't understand the situation but, looking back, I can see that he did. He knew I was short of food and that Joe and Tom tucked into his bully beef and cake out of greed, but he thought I needed their company and their 'friendship' until he finally spotted that I didn't – it was no 'friendship'.

I reckon he deliberately set about humiliating Joe and Tom, particularly Joe, since Tom didn't know his left hand from his right. Mr Blair's blue eyes would sort of gleam hard. He told Tom that he never bought more than a ha'porth of penny stamps 'to save money' and watched Tom nod dumbly. He told Joe that one of the best carpenters he knew used a rubber hammer and a left-handed screwdriver in his workshop. 'Excellent results,' he added, straight-faced. Joe's brow furrowed. Joe also fell for the one about striped paint.

The competitions Mr Blair set became fiercer and he was bending the rules, too. But then he'd soften and meander off into his imitations, which he knew amused us all. There was the Irish tramp he'd known, the one who was always knocking on the doors of convents begging 'a cup o' tay' and resisting the temptation to filch something while the nuns had their backs turned: 'T'ank God I ain't never stolen not'in' yet.' Mr Blair could also keep us absorbed for hours (I say 'hours' but he rarely idled that long, there was always work to do) with his London tramp-slang. I remember he imitated a fully dressed tramp who was bargaining with a stark-naked tramp about the price of his clothes: 'Best rig-out you ever 'ad. A tosheroon for the coat, two 'ogs for the trousers, one and a tanner for the boots, and a 'og for the cap and scarf. That's seven bob.'

To me Mr Blair came to represent 'knowledge' – and a lot else. He knew so much – in fact he told us that London cab drivers had to pass a test called 'the knowledge'. They had to know every street in London and every short-cut! Then there was 'the knowledge' of the tramps:

'If you approach a stranger and ask for twopence he can call a policeman and get you pinched for seven days for begging. But if you drone "Nearer, my God, to thee", or pretend to sell matches, you're not begging.'

I mentioned Mr Blair reading us the passage about the rats in *Gulliver's Travels*. On another occasion he was spreading his tins of bully beef and jars of jam across the kitchen table when he suddenly asked – the schoolmaster in him, I expect – which of us had read the whole book and what the plot was. From the long faces worn by Joe and Tom they clearly saw the bully beef and jam flying out of the window.

Joe's arm shot up: 'Gulliver was shipwrecked and only six inches tall when he woke up from his dream.'

'Minus five points,' Mr Blair said. Joe turned scarlet, always a happy sight.

Tom blurted out that it was the 'Lilliputs' who were only six inches tall.

'Lilliputians,' Mr Blair said. 'One point only. Alex?'

'The Lilliputians were not six inches tall,' I said.

'They were!' Joe and Tom cried in unison.

'Explain, Alex,' Mr Blair said innocently.

I say 'innocently' because all I had to do was remember what he'd told me, and me alone, while Joe and Tom were at home counting their acres.

'In Swift's day "not" also meant "not quite",' I said.

'Quite right,' Mr Blair said. 'Five points.'

The other two glowered at me, smelling a rat; they both knew I could never have got it on my own.

Mr Blair then remarked that he shared Swift's liking for numbers.

'Gulliver counts everything in sight: "The King's smith conveyed fourscore and eleven chains ... which were locked to my left leg by six and thirty padlocks ..." '

'Three hundred tailors made him a suit of clothes,' I added.

Joe and Tom were looking daggers.

'You should see Alex's arithmetic marks at school,' Joe sneered and snivelled. Then out it came. '*When* Alex went to school, that is. Before he started bunking off, weeks at a time, with inspectors looking for him and everything.'

'Yeah,' Tom said uneasily – Tom didn't exactly hold the World Record for School Attendance.

I glanced at Mr Blair nervously, but whatever he was thinking, he ignored Joe's friendly intervention.

'I was no good at maths myself,' Mr Blair said. 'But numbers,' he went on rather fiercely, 'are the grapeshot of satire. However, Swift made one mathematical mistake never discovered by the nudist pansies, nancies and sodomites who govern Literary Criticism.' Mr Blair tugged at his rope lighter and made fire, then coughed badly on the smoke. 'Swift calculated, or Gulliver calculated, how many Lilliputians might equal him in volume, and so how many times their daily diet of meat and drink he required. In those days no one told an Englishman he should be happy on vegetables alone. So.'

Mr Blair's stern eye ran from one to another of us.

'So, we will do the calculation for ourselves. All we need to know is that Gulliver was in all three dimensions twelve times larger than an adult Lilliputian.'

Mr Blair sat back and waited, drumming his fingers on his knotted stick. After a while Tom said he couldn't remember the question.

'The question,' said Mr Blair, 'is how many Lilliputians would fit into Gulliver. Twenty-five points and all the bully beef to the one who gets it right.'

Tom's face was horribly screwed up. Joe's was shiny with ambition – he was always a teacher's bum-sucker. Suddenly Tom's nerve broke with greed.

'Twelve Lilliputs,' he blurted.

'A man has *three* dimensions,' Mr Blair said.

Then Joe came up with some fantastical figure whose noughts would stretch across the duck pond.

'Minus ten points for guessing,' Mr Blair said. 'Alex?'

I said: 'One thousand seven hundred and twenty-eight Lilliputians would fit into Gulliver.'

'Why?'

'Twelve times twelve times twelve.'

He nodded. 'Swift wrote one thousand seven hundred and twenty-four. He got it wrong, you see. Or maybe his printer was careless after a night of boozing in Aldgate. Alex got it right.' He pushed the whole bully beef across to me. 'Tuck in.'

Joe jumped up, beside himself. 'You were cheating!' he yelled at me. 'He told you the answers! You don't even go to school!'

Again Mr Blair refused to rise to the bait. I politely handed the bully beef back to him.

'Divide it in four, sir. Even village idiots deserve their share.'

Joe couldn't take it. 'I warn you, Alex Jones, your rotten, crummy, stinking farm will – '

Mr Blair cut in.

'Joe,' Mr Blair said calmly, 'none of us knows what will happen tomorrow.' He reached for his rope lighter and applied it to the dead fag-end in his mouth. 'I've kept a diary throughout this war, predicting what will happen during the next few days, and I've never been right once.'

Joe sniggered nervously. Mr Blair's blue eyes remained fastened on him.

'If you really want a true picture of the future, young man, imagine a boot stamping on a human face – for ever.'

Even Tom looked nervous at that, and Joe was plainly about to wet his knickers. We didn't even finish our tea because Mr Blair had the next ordeal lined up for our uninvited guests. Picking up his haversack, he herded us out of the house and up the knoll to the ruined windmill. He certainly had a bee in his bonnet about that heap of stones, he was always prodding them with his boot as if searching for buried secrets, and he would inevitably announce that the windmill had been dynamited 'by them', by 'counter-revolutionary sabotage'.

Now he set us labouring for an hour to build up the foundations, and such was his authority that not even Joe or Tom could refuse. I had no idea what he was up to until he produced what looked like two fireworks out of his haversack. He told us they were dynamite.

'It's an experiment,' he said, 'in counter-revolutionary sabotage.'

Joe was trembling from head to toe. 'Is it dangerous?' he whimpered.

Mr Blair nodded: 'Very. Anyone who doesn't fancy it can take off.'

Joe's eyes swivelled desperately and then he was haring down the knoll and across the pasture towards the five-barred gate. Tom slowly took in the situation, like Neanderthal man studying the collar-bone of an ox, and then he, too, was off at a gallop.

I was also shaking badly but Mr Blair gave me a wink and I felt better. He told me to go and lie flat in the spinney until I'd heard the second explosion.

'The *second* one, Alex.'

'OK, sir.'

I bolted for the spinney, flattened myself behind a fallen tree trunk, buried my nose in the wet earth, covered my head with my hands, and waited – terrified that Mr Blair would blow himself to pieces. I'd really be in it with Constable Gill if that happened. I didn't own a watch, of course, but I reckoned twenty minutes had passed when I dared to lift my snout above the tree trunk. I could see Mr Blair lying flat behind a rock, about twenty paces from the windmill, bleakly studying his rope lighter and cursing softly.

Finally he stood up, his trousers soaking wet, his tweed jacket covered in moss and wet leaves, and hailed me over.

'It's the cotton,' he muttered.

I was quite glad it was. I wasn't of course aware that we had been rehearsing one of the great scenes of modern English literature – though it didn't take quite that form when it brought Mr Blair fame and fortune.

Several weeks passed. Joe and Tom came back to the farm just once more – a total, bloody disaster in fact, which I must now explain. It could never have happened when my dad was around. Though I wasn't talking to Joe and Tom much, I was often lonely on the farm and sometimes hankered after the days when we boys used to muck around together, even if there was no love lost. Being 'responsible' all of the time was a bit too much. Anyway, I stupidly fell in with Tom's Big Idea of staging a 'proper American rodeo' on Manor Farm one Saturday afternoon. Any of the village kids could come, for threepence entrance fee, and this money (Tom generously explained) would be nobly donated to 'the upkeep of Manor Farm'.

I really hate to describe what happened. In fact I won't. To begin with, most of the village boys never paid a penny, they just hopped over the fence. And soon we had our exhausted animals out, Boxer and Clover, the mare Mollie, Benjamin the donkey, with a great swarm of boys leaping on them bare-back and shouting 'Hidyho!' It was a miracle that none of them got thrown and kicked to death.

Our horses were underfed and quickly exhausted. Soon their eyes were rolling from shock and fear. They had never in all their lives been treated that way. Some idiot – almost certainly Tom Frederick – had tied a tin can and a red ribbon to Mollie's tail, and she was whinnying and tossing her head back like mad, clouds of steam rising from her flanks.

'You're not Spanish Roman Catholics!'

It was Mr Blair. Out of the blue, as if he'd dropped by parachute. (Tom later claimed that he had.) I never heard him yell before or since, he didn't have the voice for it. He was wading in among the boys, slashing with his stick in an expert way – a real, sharp swipe aimed to miss its target by inches.

'This is England!' he kept shouting, and he meant it; the younger kids took flight while the older ones, including Joe and Tom, slouched off, jeering, hands in pockets, kicking stones and threatening to throw a few in Mr Blair's direction, though they didn't. Mr Blair wasn't the type to throw stones at. As he untied the tin can from Mollie's tail she reared and kicked in a frenzy, but he didn't show any fear, he knew about horses, though you could tell that the effort he was making was hurting his chest. Gradually he calmed Mollie and then I helped him lead the horses and the donkey to their stalls.

'A nation which mistreats animals will embrace the first tinpot dictator who offers himself,' Mr Blair said.

'Yes, sir, I know, sir.'

I expected him to give me a real dressing-down but Mr Blair always understood a situation. I expect he found me rather subdued during our tea (he'd brought another feast and I wasn't sorry to be consuming Tom's and Joe's portions). He told me about going down a coal mine in Lancashire. He'd set out to find Wigan Pier but there wasn't one.

'It doesn't exist. It was once a tumble-down wooden jetty on a little muddy canal. Calling it a pier was a joke. The music-hall comedians kept the pier alive, you see. And I fell for it.'

He said the average miner was short of stature and it was

very hard going if you were tall but it was even more hard going to spend your whole life in the pits.

'Everything I have done,' he said, 'I could stop doing at a moment's notice. Very few Englishmen share that freedom. All I'm doing in life is offering the support of an irrelevant middle-class voice for those who don't have that freedom.'

He pushed the remains of the cake in my direction and settled down with his fags to watch me eat. I felt at home with him. Presently he took a paperback book from his haversack and began to turn the pages. I was watching him expectantly.

'Never lick your finger when you turn the pages of a book or magazine,' he said. 'It's a disgusting habit. It's like Yanks leaving chewing gum on a cinema seat.'

I nodded, bemused. He put his book down and slurped his black tea out of the saucer.

'You borrow a book from the library and you find the top right-hand corner of every page has been reduced to a soggy ruin. A sticky bog of germs. It's criminal, you see. It's also unhealthy because of the acid in the paper. If you read a hundred books a year, each two hundred and fifty pages long, and finger-licked every page, after forty-seven years and three months you'd be dead.'

'Really? Is that true?'

He nodded grimly. I promised never to do it.

He sighed, not entirely convinced, and opened his book again.

'A poem,' he said. Then he read a few lines, slowly, in his flat, injured voice:

'As I stand at the lichened gate
With warring worlds on either hand –

To left the black and boundless trees,
The empty sties, the barns that stand
Like tumbling skeletons – and to right
The factory towers ...'

He broke off: 'You're not listening.'

My mouth was crammed with cake. 'I am, sir. It's very good, sir. Who wrote it?'

My question seemed the right one. 'I did,' he said. 'I always wanted to be a poet, you see. But I'll never be a poet.'

'I know, sir.'

'How do you know?'

'You told me, sir. What's the poem called?'

'It's called "On a Ruined Farm Near His Master's Voice Gramophone Factory".'

I thought about this. 'It's quite a sad poem, isn't it? Will you read me the rest?'

Later he wrote a story in which our mare Mollie was so mad for red ribbons that she betrayed the Revolution. But that story is the other story.

Riding up from the five-barred gate, I spotted a smart gent standing in the yard beside a beaut. It was the last of the 4½-litre Lagonda drophead coupés. I slowed to a wobble, ready to do a bunk, but there was no way a school inspector could drive a job like that. They were Ford 8s if they were lucky. Also this gent was flapping a pair of kid gloves in his hands and you could tell that his overcoat was made to measure. Nothing off the peg here. He didn't look at home at all and his shoes, which had clearly been slaughtered in London, were carefully avoiding the puddles in the yard.

'Good morning,' he said in a very posh voice.

'Morning, sir.'

'Might you be Alex?'

Might I be? The gent looked confident but ill-at-ease. He was trying to press a steady smile into his mouth but his very large, dark eyes remained distinctly glum. He carried quite a nose which seemed to begin in the middle of his forehead and to carry on down at roughly the same angle. His ears were larger than life and the back of his head had been levelled off, it just ran straight down into his neck. His hair was very trim and brushed straight back. He was smoking out of a cigarette holder, real ivory by the look of it.

'I'm looking for our mutual friend,' he said.

I was admiring his car. 'I bet that was designed by W. O. Bentley,' I said. 'Independent front suspension, hydraulic breaks. Six-cylinder engine capable of going from seven to a hundred and three point four miles per hour without snatching.'

The gent looked impressed. In fact he was making quite a song out of looking impressed. The big sad eyes were as full of calculations as a grocer's account book.

'Like a ride?'

I didn't respond. It might be a kidnap. The man in the hat in the Ford 8 was probably lurking up the road, in Pilkington's copse.

'Quite a farm you've got here,' the gent said.

'Hm.'

'So where's our mutual friend? Had sight of him lately?'

'Who's that, then?'

'George.'

I shook my head and shrugged and wiped my nose on my sleeve.

'A very tall, thin man with big feet,' the gent said. 'From London.'

This could be Mr Blair so I went into my rustic idiot act: 'Dunno no George, 'cept a'school.'

'My name's Fred,' he said, offering me his hand. I hastily wiped mine on my shirt. Then he added a second name which began with 'war' and ended in something German by the sound of it. It was perfectly obvious to me that this gent was a German spy and was never called Fred. The next thing he said clinched it:

'George and I had some lively arguments before the war. He thought preparing for war would turn us into Fascists. Of course a Jew knew which way the wind was blowing. As soon as we were at war George blew on-course and started planting spuds and trying to get himself called up.'

I could see through all that and sniffed. My nose was always running. Mr Blair was no Jew.

'George and I are in the same Home Guard unit,' Fred said. 'I'd abandoned my uniform as a young officer at the end of the Great War – of course George was five years younger and had to sit it out at Eton, for which he never forgave himself. Anyway, I am enrolled in Sergeant Blair's section of the St John's Wood Company.'

So he did mean Mr Blair.

'That's Eric you mean, sir.'

'Ah.' Fred's cigarette holder twisted sideways. 'Yes, Eric. Looks splendid in his tricorn cap – he had to buy it himself because his head is too big for the standard issue. He falls in with the intensity of an austere Cromwellian Ironside.'

'He told us about Molotov cocktails.'

'Did he! Well, we possess one weapon of real power and utility, the spigot mortar.'

'Range four hundred yards,' I said. 'Anti-tank.'

Fred beamed. 'Don't tell me he's been demonstrating it down here?'

'Oh no. Worse luck,' I added amiably.

'I'm not sure about the "worse luck", Alex. When the spigot mortar is loaded with a live round its four legs have to be hammered into the ground to take up the recoil. George and I became pretty adept at it on the ranges at Aldershot but one day George lost concentration and didn't bother to hammer the legs in because he thought he was loading the barrel with a wooden drill bomb, which is wholly inert, no recoil. Whoof! Private Smith was unconscious for twenty-four hours while Private Jones lost all his front teeth.'

I thought about this.

'Was it Mr Blair's fault?'

Fred nodded and placed a new cigarette, taken from a slim gold case, which he snapped closed with relish, into his long ivory holder.

'George had to appear before a Court of Inquiry. Private Jones needed a new set of dentures.'

'Is Jones his real name?'

Fred shrugged. 'Smith and Jones are figures of speech.' He must have noticed my expression because he hastened to ask if my family was called Smith.

'Jones.'

'Ah. Accept my apologies. I only knew your name is Alex.'

'Who told you, then? Did Mr Blair tell you? I mean, how to get here ...'

'No, no. Oh no. He's entirely secretive.' One of Fred's large, sad eyes winked. 'I asked Eileen, as a matter of fact. She gave me your Christian name and said you were a wild boy living on a semi-abandoned farm near Porterstone. She was a bit guarded about George's new book but thought he was visiting you today.'

'Book?'

Fred nodded and slowly exhaled with some satisfaction. 'I've published two of them. I regard myself as his publisher. But Gollancz has an option on the next two fiction titles. Gollancz! That stooge of the Kremlin who abandoned his own faith. But for me *Homage* would never have seen the light of day. Yet now I can never track George down in London, a bomb destroyed my entire paper ration in Plymouth, and Eileen thinks George is here, which you say he isn't, so maybe he's not playing it quite straight at home, which does surprise me though not entirely after what he told me about certain incidents in Marrakesh. Hmmm ...'

I couldn't make head or tail of all that.

'Maybe you're looking for someone else?' I suggested.

'Else?'

'Yes, sir. I told you, sir. My friend's called Eric.'

Fred smiled knowingly. 'Bullet scar on his neck?'

'Yes, sir.'

'Rolls his own fags and lights them from a rope because the U-boats will sink our supply of Scandinavian matchwood? Nothing cheers him up like imminent catastrophe?'

'He didn't exactly say that.'

'Admires Kipling and – heaven preserve us – Gissing?'

Fred grabbed me in a friendly way and sort of shortened his legs – he couldn't exactly kneel in the filthy puddles of the yard – to bring his odd nose level with mine.

'What's he writing, Alex?' Fred whispered with amazing intensity. 'Has he shown you any of it? Read you any chapters? Pigs, is it? You must tell me.'

If there was one law of life it was never to tell any adult

what you 'must' tell them. Anyway, Mr Blair never bent his knees or pretended to come down on the same level, or said one 'must' tell him anything. I didn't see how this German Jew spy could be a friend of Mr Blair's, even though Tom Frederick was convinced Mr Blair himself was a spy of sorts, and Constable Gill was still 'on the lookout' for him.

'Are you a German spy, sir?'

Slowly he straightened his legs. Nice trousers, I thought.

'Alex, this island of ours is a precious stone set in a silver sea.' Then he took a printed card from his crocodile-skin wallet and gravely handed it to me.

'I want you to notify me as soon as George finishes his pig-book.'

'Wouldn't that make *me* a spy?'

'No, a scout. A publisher's scout. It's for George's sake, Alex. He's heading straight back into the Soviet conspiracy. Gollancz! Don't you want to help your friend?'

'But he – '

'You mustn't tell him I was here.' Fred's gloved finger lay across his lips and his eyes seemed sadder than ever. He was now holding a ten-shilling note in his hand. 'You know how to make a reverse-charge phone call?'

I stared at him. He sighed.

'Have you ever made a phone call, Alex?'

'No, sir.'

'You cycle to the Post Office. You lift the receiver. You dial – ' Fred gave up. The ten shillings went back into his wallet and the Lagonda bumped carefully down the rutted track to the five-barred gate. My unclean hand held a shilling, which wasn't bad.

I thought I might keep quiet about Fred, if it meant more

shillings, but the next time Mr Blair showed up it came straight out.

'Is Fred a German Jew spy, sir?'

'Who?'

'The gent in the Lagonda, sir. "Our mutual friend", he called you.'

Mr Blair stood like a blasted tree. 'How did he find his way here?'

I'd not seen him so vexed. He kept thudding his big boot against the corrugated iron wall of the sties, glowering at Napoleon and Snowball as if they were somehow mixed up in it. Obviously he was keeping his visits to the farm secret from his friends in London.

'Fred said a lady told him how to get here, sir. He said the lady thought you were here when you weren't ...'

'Eileen?'

'I don't remember, sir.' (Though I did.)

'Did he mention Connolly?' I shook my head. 'I suspect Fred of comparing me adversely to Connolly, the prophet of the sluttish antinomians.' I gaped. Mr Blair glanced down at me suspiciously. 'You're not a covert antinomian, are you?'

I grinned and nodded.

'Or a Burnhamite, hm?'

'A what?'

'A clandestine disciple of James Burnham, apostle of the managerial revolution. Burnham's fascinated by power in any shape or form. He believes Communism, Fascism and the New Deal are all variants of the unstoppable, inevitable managerial revolution. Do you agree with that?'

'Definitely! Smack on!'

'Hm. Fred pretends to support my view of Burnham, but

publishers are all swindlers, aren't they? Burnham's main message is that the winners will win.'

I pondered this. 'Like Arsenal, you mean? Or Len Hutton?'

Mr Blair gradually calmed down. We were out in the long pasture because he had this idea that he could feel each ewe and tell whether she was going to have twins, in which case he painted a kind of '2' on her rump, though it looked more like a 'z' or half of a swastika.

'I quite like Fred,' he said. 'He's a rare thing, a Warburg without money.'

'What – with a $4\frac{1}{2}$-litre Lagonda!'

'His grandfather amassed wealth out of the Tuppenny Tube but his father refused to work and frittered it away. When I first met him Fred was flirting with Trotskyism – like Snowball over there – but it was probably his way of getting at Gollancz.'

'Do you have a car, sir?'

'Couldn't possibly afford it.'

'Not even a Morris 8 or Austin 7?'

'Money's better spent on books.'

'When I grow up I might have the 1939 18/85 Wolseley. Or a Buick V-8 – it's rated at 22 hp. Did you know that Humfrey, that's spelt with an f, Symons was driving a V-8 when he broke the London–Cape record in a time of thirty-one days twenty-two hours despite falling through a bridge in the ... Kogo.'

'The Congo?'

I nodded.

'It belongs to the King of Belgium. Who's a Nazi collaborator.'

'What belongs to him – the Wolseley V-8?'

'The Congo.'

We had reached the house now and it was definitely time for tea. Mr Blair carefully cleaned his paintbrush, having turned our flock of swastikaed ewes into Nazi collaborators.

'So what did Fred Warburg want to find out, hm?'

'He said he should publish you. He looked a bit of a Yid spiv to me.'

'Anti-semitism is a crime, Alex. A Jew is a Jew, not a "Yid". Right?'

'Sorry. My dad said – '

'The Warburgs have included some of the richest men in the world, you see. Money-changers once, then bankers. M. M. Warburg & Sons of Hamburg. In 1804 Napoleon besieged Hamburg and kidnapped one of Fred's ancestors as a hostage.'

'Why?'

'Ransom money.'

'But you said Fred doesn't have much money, sir.'

'I'm talking about Fred's ancestor in Napoleon's time. When was Napoleon?'

'Same time as Nelson, who did him in.'

'When was Nelson?'

'Same time as Boney.' But I was thinking about Fred. 'If Fred's from Hamburg, he could be a German spy.'

'Fred is an English gentleman born and bred. Westminster and Christ Church.'

'But those are churches, aren't they? How can a Y— . . . I mean a Jew . . .'

The kettle began to hum and a tin of Spam came out of Mr Blair's haversack.

CHAPTER V

Shortly after I gave up school altogether Mr Blair brought me a tin of Cadbury's hot chocolate. He said Fry's was second-best. I bunked school entirely because I knew they were waiting to grab me, to take me 'in', whereas on the farm you could hear a car approaching a mile away and even though the man in the hat once tried it in the middle of the night, parking his Ford 8 beyond the five-barred gate and creeping up on foot, the dogs set up a shindy and I sent Jessie and Bluebell straight for him while making myself scarce. On that occasion the man departed but the hat, or chewed bits of it, stayed behind. I gave it to our pig Squealer, who fancied himself in it.

Did I mention that I also suffered the unwelcome attentions of our vicar, the Reverend Goodfellow, a do-gooder of about thirty approaching ninety, suffering a bad shoulder from El Alamein, or some such excuse – and dead set to enlist me among his choirboys? Too poor for a Ford 8, he'd slither up to the yard on his bicycle, desperate to save my soul but never finding it, retreating from the attentions of Jessie and Bluebell with shredded trousers while I made myself scarce in the barn.

Mr Blair also gave me a shilling, on top of the Cadbury's.

'Being poor's nothing to be proud of but it's nothing to be ashamed of either,' he said.

He didn't mention Tom and Joe, nor did I, but he definitely understood – though I didn't bother to inform him how Joe had brought me an invitation to tea from Ma Pilkington, and how I'd said 'OK, thanks', making note of Joe's shifty gaze, and how I'd taken care to cross the fields of Foxwood Farm, surveying the house from the shelter of a copse, rather than cycling up the baronial drive that led to 'Belle Vue' – and there sure enough tucked into the garage at the back was the Ford 8 belonging to the man-without-the-hat. So I lay low all through tea-time, my stomach twitching for the grub Lady P. would have laid on before handing me over, and she herself periodically tottering out on to the drive in her high heels, twittering 'I do wonder where that Alex has got to! Oh that boy', and then the man-in-the-new-hat drove away and soon it was dark and I catapulted my best stone, my cannonball, polished like a prize conker, through the living-room (sorry, drawing-room) window. There was a hue and cry, of course, the dogs were out, but you only had to wade the shallow stream below the copse to lose them.

Soon after that I received a letter written in capitals but covered in Joe's thumbprints (strawberry jam by the look of it): 'WHOS DRUNK DAD DID HISSELF IN AFTER GETTING TITTS ELLEN PREG. A FREND.' I brooded on this. I'd noticed that my dad's best shotgun had gone missing with my dad. But nothing Joe Pilkington said could be true.

Now that Joe and Tom had made themselves scarce from Manor Farm, Mr Blair began to speak to me in a different way – his tone was gentler – or perhaps I imagined it. Walking across the pasture, swinging his knotted stick, he said:

'Alex, it's a myth that country people don't love nature. Medieval literature, including the popular ballad, is full of an almost Georgian enthusiasm for nature.'

I never quite understood 'Georgian'. There were so many Georges and I knew that our King, George VI, had succeeded his father, George V, but after a short gap called Edward VIII which no one, my parents included, would talk about. My stamp album showed George V with a beard. In later years I realised that George V's father also had a beard and was called Edward VII. I had thought they were the same King because our King George VI didn't have a beard. Nor did Mr Blair, so it was a puzzle whenever he described himself as 'a hopeless old Edwardian' – and even more of a puzzle when he called the writers of his own childhood 'Georgians'.

He was very keen on history. I already mentioned what he said about the 'English Revolution', which was obviously Cavaliers and Roundheads. To listen to him, you'd believe he'd fought for both sides, striding from one end of the battlefield to the other. It may have been the same thing in Spain – he told me he'd enlisted for 'the Republic', fought for 'the Poom' (this turned out to be 'POUM'), and then had been 'silenced and censored by Loyalist lackeys', the worst of whom was 'King Martin, the New Statesman'. I mentioned to him that Joe Pilkington claimed to know the kings and queens of England since William the Conqueror. Mr Blair replied that the real kings were 'landlords, industrialists and bankers'. He offered to take me to see the Bank of England and the Stock Exchange after the war. I asked him whether they were anywhere near the Tower of London (I'd made a model of it from a cardboard kit, but none of the Bank or the Stock) and he said it was impossible to get in because of 'the Yanks'.

I told him that according to Miss Symes, who taught us English, history, geography, drawing, nature, arithmetic and PT, but in practice nothing at all because she was quite young and good-looking, though not in Ellen's class, English history began in 1066. (I didn't mention that I hadn't caught sight of Miss Symes for some weeks, nor she me.)

'Well,' he said, 'that's an improvement on Queen Boadicea with a Union Jack draped over her chariot.'

'Wasn't she real, then, sir?'

'Real or not, the Union Jack dates from 1714.'

Mr Blair said that the Pope of Rome had dressed down William the Conk (Mr Blair used a long word beginning with 'ex') because he'd married his cousin, Mathilda. Mr Blair said that William and Mathilda could only get out of this fix by building huge churches and starting up two big charity hospitals, one for men (Mr Blair said 'omm') and one for women ('dum'), in the middle of 'Con' – where there was going to be one hell of a battle in a few months' time.

'Is it still the same town as in 1066?' I asked.

He nodded. 'Con. C-a-e-n.'

'You told Joe we can never be sure what's going to happen next,' I objected.

'I'll bet you sixpence on Caen,' Mr Blair said. 'It will be us, the Yanks, the French, the Poles and the Canadians, all against Fritz. And if that doesn't sound fair you'd better know that when William the Conk assembled his invasion army at Dives, it wasn't only Normans, but also mercenaries from all over the place.'

We were walking across the pasture, just the two of us.

Mr Blair advised me never to believe that 'being thoroughly miserable about everything is progressive.'

I asked him what it meant.

'It should mean making a fairer world.'

'What's unfair, sir?'

He stopped and surveyed me from his great height.

'So you have no complaints, Alex?'

I told him how my dad had tried to do away with himself after my mum discovered him with Ellen in the hayloft, by swallowing meths, I said, and that was why they'd taken him away. Mr Blair sort of nodded. I'd lost count of the different stories I'd told him about my dad – though probably Mr Blair hadn't. I think he was embarrassed. He never liked to talk about particular people or particular feelings you might have. When he was embarrassed he would always do something with his hands, carving things with his big pen-knife and lost in his own thoughts. He made a small chair which wouldn't stand up. Any kind of effort took it out of him, his movements became slow and deliberate, but he kept forcing himself, he couldn't be idle.

'They kept testing me for TB,' he muttered shyly. 'But the tests were negative.' I thought this must mean 'bad', but then he added: 'So it seems I'm in the clear on that.'

Using his hands didn't stop him talking, though. It was while he was making the chair which wouldn't stand up that he told me about a cripple he'd known, Bozo, a very fine pavement artist who was quite educated and had lived in Paris. Bozo had had an accident, falling forty feet on to one foot. A doctor had told him he was lucky not to have fallen on to both feet. 'You'd have shut up like a bloody concertina,' the doctor had said. 'Your thigh bones would be sticking out of your ears.'

Mr Blair chuckled faintly. I said I was surprised a doctor spoke quite like that, even a French one.

'He probably didn't,' Mr Blair said. 'It's Bozo telling the story to me and me to you – you see. A wonderful story-teller, Bozo. He'd been to India, you know, and watched them cremating a corpse – that's burning it on a heap of faggots, because there are just too many people in India for decent burial. Anyway, according to Bozo, after the heat gets up the corpse starts kicking –'

'Kicking! He was still alive!'

'No, just muscular reflex to intense heat. Bozo said it gave him "quite a turn". He said the corpse "wriggled about like a kipper on hot coals", and then the belly blew up and went off with a bang.'

'Ugh!'

'Well, that's Bozo's gift for images, you see. It all depends who's telling the story, doesn't it?' He regarded me. 'See, Alex, if you were telling a story about a farm ... well, let's say some strange events on a farm ... who would tell the story?'

'I would, sir, if I was telling it.'

He nodded. 'Yes. But you could arrange for one of the characters to tell the story, couldn't you? Or no one at all.'

'No one, sir?'

'"One night the cunning fox crept towards the farm. He had his eye on the chicken-run and his ear cocked for sounds of the farmer. But the farmer had drunk five pints of ale and was fast asleep in bed." Right? So who's telling it?'

'The author is.'

'Not in my view. If I write a book about things that happened to me in Burma or Spain, then I, Geo— ... then I, Eric Blair, am telling it. But if I make up a story and things just happen, like the fox creeping up on the chickens, then no one is telling it.' A pause. 'You see.'

I didn't. I knew by now I could risk arguing with him. He was the only grown-up I'd ever known who actually wanted you to answer back if you wanted to. So I said that if strange things were happening on a farm it would be better if the farmer told the story, or maybe the farmer's son – better than no one.

'Not with a fable,' he said. Then he said something odd: 'Do you think one can die if one has an unwritten book in one's mind?'

I couldn't answer but I felt sad.

'Anyway,' he muttered, 'there's to be no biography of me. It's in my will.'

'What's a biography?'

'Someone tells a pack of lies about your life. Some charlatan.'

That was the day I finally dared ask about the scar on his neck.

'A Fascist sniper in Spain,' he said. 'Just a single shot. I'd stood up above the parapet like a damn fool. The doctors told me that if the bullet had been a millimetre to the left I would have been dead.'

He was quite matter-of-fact about it, as if it had happened to someone else.

'It was a normal seven-millimetre bore, copper-plated Spanish Mauser bullet, fired from a distance of a hundred and seventy-five yards. At that range it still carried a velocity of six hundred feet per second and a cauterising temperature. I had no voice at all. It came back after electrotherapy, but low and hoarse. Didn't you notice?'

'No, sir. Well . . .'

Mr Blair mentioned that he could 'get by' in a number of languages, Urdu for example, and that he'd 'picked up enough Catalan' to be made a corporal or *cabo*.

'That meant I had to get up early to turn out the guard, not my cup of tea. There was one chap there who called me a "cool customer" because I used to creep over the parapet and see how close I could get to the Fascist lines. His name was Donovan, an Irishman of course, and we shared a dugout. He used to complain that I'd kill him with my black tobacco smoke long before the Fascists did.'

Mr Blair chuckled and wheezed. 'Paddy Donovan.'

Then he told me how a lot of the shells never exploded and how each side kept firing them back and forth like 'pass the parcel'. The worst problem was the lice in his trousers. Mr Blair then threw me a look and shyly mentioned his wife:

'Eileen came out to Spain. She visited me at the front. She did a wonderful job, coping with everything. She seemed to enjoy it.'

I could tell he was waiting to see whether I'd show any interest in his wife – he probably knew that boys never acknowledge the existence of females, but in fact I felt a bit disappointed about his wife.

'We don't have any children,' he said. 'When I came back from Spain I saw English railway-cuttings smothered in wild flowers, great horses like your Boxer browsing in deep meadows, larkspurs in the cottage gardens, posters telling of cricket matches and royal weddings ... the milk on the doorstep every morning, the *New Statesman* out every Friday. Spain was nowhere on the horizon and as for Wigan Pier –'

'Which doesn't exist!'

'Wigan was just a smudge of smoke and misery hidden

from our little arcadia by the curve of the earth's surface.'

I absorbed this. If he was telling me I was living in a cottage garden and playing cricket all day, I wasn't buying it. But here again he was a step ahead of me:

'Of course there's no milk on your doorstep, Alex. It's us adults who landed you kids in this war. One day we'll have to do something good for a change.' His thoughts then went their own way: 'What is anarchy, Alex?'

I didn't know the word.

'It's order carried to excess,' he said. 'Like my father and his generation.'

I asked about his father. It was better than asking about his wife.

'I was born Eric Arthur Blair in Bengal on 25 June 1903, the son of Richard Walmesley Blair, who was working for the Opium Department of the Government of India.'

'What's opium?'

'It's a drug. Useful in medicines – morphine – but that wasn't the imperial game, medicines. Trade was the game: addiction. Human wrecks. When he retired my father came home from India – I hadn't seen him for years – and set up as secretary of the Harpsden golf club. He'd been "Indian Civil", you see. He didn't want me to go to Oxford, he wanted me to shoot an elephant. When my father died I closed his eyes in the traditional way by putting pennies on his eyelids. After the funeral I didn't know what to do with the two pennies. I couldn't put them back in my pocket, could I?'

'I don't know, sir.'

'In the end I walked down to the sea and threw them in.' He studied me. 'Where do you think my father's soul is now?'

That didn't seem to demand an answer. Mr Blair had taken

a breather from the chair which wouldn't stand up and was stroking our dachshund, Charles, who my mum had wanted to take with her to Porterstone but old Ma Pyke said 'no animals, no pets'. Charles never lost any time in leaping into Mr Blair's lap, scrounging for titbits. Mr Blair called him Charlatan, I don't know why, but the name stuck like all his names.

'My mother also liked dachshunds,' Mr Blair said. 'They always attended her breakfast in bed. She loved them more than her children though probably she didn't know it. Perhaps she did. She liked red-and-white curtains, a well-kept garden, dogs on the lawn. When she died in hospital I found a copy of *Homage to Catalonia* beside her bed, you see.'

There was a long silence.

'A copy of what, sir?'

'But the pages didn't look turned,' he said. 'The book one's mother has bought but hasn't read ... perhaps I ought to have given her a copy.'

I understood that he was telling these things to me and me alone. So I told him about how my dad had taken Tom Frederick's dad to court after his cows broke through our thorn hedge and ate all the clover in our pasture. But the judge wasn't on our side and said it was my dad's responsibility to keep his hedges in good order, or some such, and so my dad lost money on the case and began drinking more and shouting at my mum and then he went after our Land Girl, Ellen.

Mr Blair listened in his half-here, half-there way. He didn't say anything but about eighteen months later, when the book arrived, I found my dad described as a drunkard and Tom's dad as 'a tough, shrewd man, perpetually involved in lawsuits and with a name for driving hard bargains'. The Fredericks were furious when they read this and put it around the village that this Blair man, or whatever he called himself, must have got it from me, and they would have sued Mr Blair if they could have proved whatever you have to prove, which they couldn't, because I wasn't a 'truthful witness' or whatever.

I felt very let down by Mr Blair but some years later, with my memory tracking back and back over the same ground, I realised that he'd sort of warned me, when he and I were alone on the farm – warned me about himself. It's difficult to describe how he did it because he had this way of saying one thing when he meant another. His remark about the 'human fox', for instance. I haven't mentioned the fact that soon after he first showed up at the farm he gave me a copy of a story called *Dr Jekyll and Mr Hyde.* I remember it was Halloween, because Mr Blair was carving spooky masks out of turnips, lighting candles (he was very fond of candles), and generally scaring the wits out of us boys down at the spinney, though of course a bonfire by night was not on in those days. I liked the pictures in *Dr Jekyll* but found the book slow going – I preferred the Hyde bits.

Several months passed and he never asked me about the book, but now, when we were together on the farm in midwinter, and I was telling him about my dad's lawsuit with Frederick, he led the way into the farmhouse kitchen, put the kettle on the stove and asked me whether I'd read the book.

I admitted I'd liked the Hyde bits best.

'Of course Stevenson was Scotch,' Mr Blair said. 'I've no time for the Scotch. People sometimes assume my name is Scotch but it isn't.' He glowered as if waiting for me to tell him it was. 'The Scotchification of England,' he continued, 'has been going on for these last fifty years. Gordon, Colin, Malcolm, Donald – and what about Alec and Alex? – these are the gifts of Scotland to the world, along with golf, whisky, porridge and the work of Barrie and Stevenson.'

I said I wasn't Scotch.

'That's my point,' he said. 'Jones? Sounds Welsh, doesn't it. Even the Welsh are Scotch now.' He must have seen my anger rising – in our circle 'to welsh' meant to betray someone and a Welshman was some kind of shifty tinker with the gift of the gab. Mr Blair guided our thoughts back to Robert Louis Stevenson.

'The Scotch are Puritans,' he said, 'and your Puritan has no imagination for sin, none at all, because he believes sin is everyone other than himself. Hypocrites, the Scotch. They were the worst planters in Burma. Humbugs, you see. Stevenson's Hyde-figure is frankly a bore, isn't he?'

'Why, sir?'

'Because all he does is prowl the streets of London by night, molesting and murdering. And because he commits his foul crimes under the influence of a magic potion which changes not only his character but his identity.'

I didn't follow. 'But that's the story, sir.'

'To me the most interesting crimes are the ones I commit without swallowing any magic potion.'

'You, sir? Crimes?'

Mr Blair poured scalding water into the pot, swirled it round, emptied it out, heaped in his usual mound of black tea leaves, covered them with boiling water (it had to be still boiling), put the lid on the pot, and looked at me as if he'd never seen me before.

'Let's take Dr Jekyll. All he has to do, to become a genuine criminal, is to write up his medical case-histories by night, betraying confidentiality between doctor and patient, and then publish them under the name of Hyde – with a few additional, imaginative touches – and there you have it: a bona fide criminal concealed within an honest doctor of medicine.'

I didn't know that those fierce blue eyes and ravaged cheeks belonged to both the Doctor and the Mister. And when, later, I did know, I began to put it the other way round. It was the criminal who was writing stories under the name of the good doctor. It was the body-snatcher, the prowling spy of the night, who was offering his corpses to the world as miracles of surgical dissection.

Still later, I asked myself why Mr Blair had stubbornly employed a word which is properly applied only to sticky tape, beef and whisky. I think Mr Blair said 'Scotch' because ordinary Englishmen said 'Scotch'. This most special of men couldn't bear to be anything special.

CHAPTER VI

I got a letter from my mum, the first I'd ever had from her and I didn't even recognise her handwriting. She was 'quite well' again, 'despite everything', and back with Ma Pyke, and she wanted me back in the damp attic with one bed. I put the letter in my bedroom drawer underneath Ellen's pink envelope. I was having certain sensations at night, more truthfully at dawn, and they were always to do with Ellen. In one dream Ellen came back to live on the farm with me and we were rolling in the hay when my dad walked in and crumbled into small pieces of charred pork. I was spending a lot of time with the pigs so I suppose that was it. How could I know that Ellen would indeed come back – though not quite as I had imagined?

Her full name was Ellen Cripps. Her father was a gentleman with a house in London. I was told that he had evacuated his family on the outbreak of war. Ellen came to us through Cripps's friendship with the Pilkingtons. I remembered how Cripps had brought her down in an 18 hp Wolseley, he all dressed up as an officer with pips on his shoulders and parachute wings on his lapel. She looked very much the young lady who'd never got dirt under her painted fingernails –

but I liked her at once. My dad had looked sceptical and my mum daggers, but Cripps had graciously explained that his daughter wanted 'to do her bit' and he was prepared to subsidise her wages. My dad's scowl softened, though my mum's didn't. Major Cripps was invited in for a cup of tea and said what a splendid farm, jolly good effort, and Ellen said what a cosy little house. I was standing in the kitchen staring at her like a love-struck fool when she gave me a flashing smile, asked me my name and said:

'You'll have to show me the ropes, Alex.'

Then Major Cripps drove away, waving. According to rumour, he was having a 'good war'.

But that was all years ago.

A woman was now bicycling towards the farmhouse. It was the first time my mum had come near the farm. The dogs swarmed round in greeting but you'd have thought they were savaging her from her long-suffering expression. The dachshund Charles went mad but she scarcely fondled him. She did look better but my filthy appearance clearly upset her. She'd brought a small bag of food but now she gazed at the house with loathing:

'I'm not going in there.'

I shrugged. 'Why not? It's not very clean but it's OK.'

She went in and started scrubbing everything in sight and demanding to know where I'd got my tins of food and jars of jam, some of which she recognised as Ma Pyke's.

'You never give me any money,' I said. 'Even when they took you away you didn't leave anything.' Of course I knew that she'd been trying to squeeze me till hunger drove me back to Ma Pyke's, but I could see she was shaken by what I'd said.

'Here's a shilling,' she said, poking in her purse. 'I'm not made of money, you know. So who's this gentleman I hear so much about, this Mr Blair?'

I shrugged. 'He doesn't come often.'

'Oh yes – and why does he come at all?'

'He helps me on the farm and – '

'And what?'

'He brings me food.'

'Because your mother doesn't feed you properly? Because you never come near her – is that it? And what's in it for him, this gentleman of yours?'

I shrugged. 'Dunno.'

'You're not stupid, are you, Alex?'

'He's my friend.'

'Friend? How old is he, this Mr Blair?'

'Dunno.' (I'd never considered his age – everyone over twenty looked old to me.)

'Does he touch you, then?'

'No!'

'Never touch you?'

'No!'

'You're lying, aren't you? You're a born liar, aren't you? Next time, you send him packing, right?'

I was silent. She sighed.

'I'm back with Mrs Pyke. I had a turn, that's all. You haven't been to school for weeks.'

'If I'd gone they'd have taken me in.'

'Who told you that?' But she spoke without conviction. 'Won't you come and live with me like a good son should? And go to school, normal? What have I done to deserve you, eh?'

'I'm looking after the farm. No one else is.'

'The Head has promised me you won't get a thrashing ... seeing as I had a bad turn.'

'Don't care what he does.'

She sighed. 'We can't keep the farm, Alex. Pilkington came to see me. "I'd be doing you a favour, Mrs Jones," he said, smooth as oil. "Every week you hang on to the farm its value diminishes." '

'What's that mean?'

'It means falls. Time you went to school.'

I could imagine Pilkington climbing back into his 1,172cc Model C Ten, with Joe lounging in the front seat, his curls all smarmed down like Little Lord Fauntleroy.

'Where's dad?' I said.

'Don't ever ask me that again!'

To please her I showed up at school, took the thrashing I wasn't supposed to get, then skipped. The lambing season had begun, and I was often up half the night, falling into an exhausted sleep before dawn. Old Ted Hare had his 'rooms' and the lambing was too much for him. Mostly he sat in the kitchen giving me unwanted advice.

Tom and Joe were keeping their distance. During those bitter weeks of winter the only two-legged creatures I ever saw on the farm – unless you count Ted – were the strangers in black hats and smart overcoats, measuring our fields, shaking their heads over the state of the sties and stables, pocketing broken tiles from the farmhouse roof, tearing off strips of rotten wood from window sills. They laughed at my filthy appearance and foulest oaths, called me 'the wild one', looked less sure of themselves when I produced my air gun, then drove away in their 10 hp 4-door Hillman Minx saloons and their Series I Morris 8s. To report to Pilkington or Frederick.

Mr Blair found me one Saturday afternoon in the long pasture, in an utterly exhausted and filthy condition, struggling with a ewe bearing twins. One of their heads was pointing the wrong way. Mr Blair immediately pulled off his old tweed jacket, rolled up his sleeves, and set to work. Later he produced some tins from his haversack and lit a fire to get the stove going with what remained of our beech logs. (He liked gazing into fires, absorbed by the way sticks keep their shape even when reduced to glowing white ash.) The lack of a fire was I suppose the main reason why the winter seemed so cold and I couldn't stop shivering at night, no matter how many blankets I piled on my bed. Mr Blair got the stove going and boiled the kettle, and then I told him about Ellen.

When Ellen first came to the farm she complained that there was no mirror in her bedroom. She wanted a full-length one. 'Some people don't know there's a war on,' my mum said. Ellen always wore coloured ribbons in her hair and she had the sweetest tooth on the farm. She regularly pilfered my mum's hoardings from the larder. 'Doesn't she know,' my mum would curse, 'the sugar ration is down from twelve ounces a week to eight? But save enough to make a cake and *she's* straight into it!'

'Just like Mollie,' Mr Blair said.

I must have looked puzzled.

'Your mare Mollie', he said. 'Always cadging sugar lumps from my pocket.'

I told him how I'd found Ellen with my dad in the hay loft. But I didn't mention how, a week or so earlier, I'd been teasing Ellen, giving her cheek, and she'd chased me into the barn and thrown me down in the hay. She was a smasher from a posh family and I'd never felt a woman's tits pressing into me. She sat on my chest and made me say Uncle, though

I didn't because I wanted to keep her there. So now, a week or so later, I was coming to look for her because I'd caught sight of her tripping into the barn – I didn't know my dad was already in there. I only heard them. I didn't dare get too close.

'They never saw me,' I told Mr Blair.

'I dare say they wouldn't have noticed King Kong. They were making hay, you see. The Germans always attack France in the hour after lunch when the French are making hay.'

'Sir?'

'It's an expression.'

'If only my dad had been quiet about it . . . the hay-making . . . but what I couldn't stomach was his moaning like that. I didn't think men moaned.'

'You were jealous, perhaps?'

'Me!'

Then – but I didn't mention this to Mr Blair – I was running across the yard to the house, with a voice in my head saying 'Don't, don't, don't' and I swear I had a vision of everything that would happen if I did, even the farm deserted and ruined.

'So what did you do?' Mr Blair asked.

'Do? Nothing. My dad had told me to look at the rabbit traps. That's what I did.'

'So how did your mother find out?'

'Dunno. I never said she found out.'

'The best stories are ninety per cent oak and ten per cent varnish. You see.'

So I told him. Mr Blair had the knack of making you feel ashamed of lying.

My mother looked up from her work. Before the war things had been duller – my memories were clear, I'd been eight when war was declared, maybe nine when our first Land Girls had arrived. After Sunday dinner my parents would sit either side of the fireplace, working their way through the papers.

'Yards of smutty print, murders and more murders, until one or both fell asleep,' Mr Blair cut in. 'Then they snored.'

When my dad's mouth dropped open he'd begin to snore at once, but with my mum all you'd hear was an occasional sighing sound, as if she was dreaming of her discontents but not minding them too much. That was about the time when she couldn't have the baby. I remember she'd wanted a girl, because I'd refused to learn to knit, one plain, two purl, drop one ... all of that. She said a boy was no less a boy for learning to 'be useful', but I knew that it was some kind of companionship she was after. My dad probably knew as much because he always said, 'Have a go, boy,' when the knitting came up, though it came with a small wink.

Mr Blair was listening intently. 'So you ran in from the yard? What next?'

' "So what's got into you?" my mum said. "Don't you wipe your feet?" '

She was at the big kitchen table, her hands and forearms covered with flour, rolling out a lump of dough. The kitchen seemed even bigger than it was and for some reason I saw it for the first time.

'Saw it?' Mr Blair asked. 'You mean this beam across the ceiling, this stone floor with your dad's cellar underneath? He used to carry his pint mug down to the barrel in the cellar, didn't he? There was always froth on his lips when he came back up, isn't that it? And they were always arguing, your parents, over how much he'd had? That's why you now saw the kitchen for the first time – he wouldn't be going down and up to the cellar any more, not after you had said your say? And where were you standing in your muddy boots? By the big stone sink which has an iron pump instead of a tap? Could you feel the heat from the range – I expect it must burn half a ton a month?'

I gazed at Mr Blair.

I don't want to give the wrong impression. Writing all this down it sounds – I mean it sounds as if his tone of voice was like one of those law-prosecutors you see in films. But he wasn't like that – I'd say he sounded more like a man who wanted to add thoughts of his own into my story. It was only years later, when I'd begun to read his novels, I mean his earlier ones, that I understood.

'Dad's with Ellen in the barn,' I said.

My mum put down her rolling pin carefully.

'So whose business is that?' she said.

'I thought you'd want to know.'

'Maybe you think too much,' she said and, picking up the rolling pin again, she came towards me.

I bolted for my room.

'But plastered your face against the window?' Mr Blair cut in. 'You watched your mum walking slowly across the yard towards the barn. She was still wearing her house slippers despite the mud. She never ordinarily walked out in her slippers, right? She had the rolling pin in her right hand?'

I nodded.

'In her right hand or her left?'

'Dunno.'

'But she was carrying it? You're sure?'

I shrugged.

'You couldn't see because your hot breath was misting up the window?'

I said: 'She'd never wanted the Land Girls. "There'll be trouble," she often said.'

Mr Blair sighed. 'It's no fun being right.'

He was having a good smoke with his strong tea and resting comfortably and not coughing so much. Then he carefully re-tied his bootlaces as if planning to leave.

'So she found your dad with Mollie?'

'Ellen.'

'I suppose they could count themselves lucky, your dad and Ellen, to have shared a moment's joy. Lucky to have a roof over their heads and warm hay under their bums. That would strike most of the poorer city people as paradise. I could tell you about the discomforts of having a girl in the park in mid-winter. A decent working girl. Not creatures like your Mollie.'

'Ellen. I liked her. She played French cricket with me.'

'Your Ellen,' he said, rolling a fag, 'she probably models herself on American films and magazines. Heroines have to look like egg-timers or cylinders depending on the fashion. That type of girl would sell herself to any American soldier for a pair of nylons.'

'Oh no!'

'The more that sort fuss about their faces and figures, the less they want to have children.'

'No, she – '

'I had a little trollop in Paris I picked up in a café. She had a figure like a boy and an Eton crop. She had an Arab lover. They made off with my baggage and money. When I came to write about it I said the money was stolen by an Italian with side-whiskers. Less compromising, I thought – I may have been thinking of my family.'

'But Ellen wasn't – '

'Women who think about scanty panties all the time never have a comfortable fire burning in the hearth, or a dog or a cat or a parrot. You see. Or a canary.'

'But Ellen was always spoiling our dogs and cats.'

'Mind you, married women only have themselves to blame. They let themselves go after getting their man to the altar, they let their youth, looks and energy vanish overnight. They dream of nothing but marriage but as soon as they're married they do nothing but complain. It's in the culture, you see: radiant brides but no happy wives. That's why the sop stories never get beyond the "I do".'

'Do you mean my mum?'

'I don't expect she'd approve of me. I dare say you know that and don't tell her much about your friend from London. Boys are shrewd judges of adults. But are Americans adults?'

'Americans?'

'Of course you never see Yanks around Porterstone, the countryside is too hilly for air bases and your neck of the woods is too distant from the build-up for the landings in France. The other day I was challenged by a couple of fighting drunk Yanks sprawling across the counter of my local tobacconist's.'

'What happened?'

'Did you know, Alex, that an American soldier's pay is five times that of a British soldier?'

'No, sir.'

'I dare say your Land Girl Mollie ran off with some American after your mother chucked her out.'

'Her name's Ellen,' I said. 'Mollie's our mare.'

'I expect she spends all her time at the pictures, chewing gum and cadging nylons. "Movies." Exit literature. Mind you, there's a kind of soggy attraction about those padded seats in the warm, smoke-scented darkness, despite the flickering drivel on the screen. Did you know that most Americans believe that the USA suffered more casualties during the last war than we did? All this calls for some plain speaking, don't you think?'

I had fallen into a sullen silence.

'But no sensible person wants to whip up Anglo-American jealousy, do they?' he said.

I told him that Ellen's father was a Major Cripps and a gentleman – I'd met him.

'Probably a colonel by now,' Mr Blair said. 'I dare say he'd pay a few pounds for your farm.'

My thoughts reeled. 'Cripps isn't a farmer, sir.'

'Makes no difference. Is he related to Sir Stafford Cripps?'

'Who?'

'The Socialist. The Government sent him out to talk to the Indians. Waste of time.'

Mr Blair poured us more black tea topped up with the thick farm milk from our two remaining Jersey cows.

'So what do they tell you about the facts of life nowadays? Does the doctor bring the baby in the black bag?'

'Sir?'

'Hats off to the factory lad who with fourpence in the world puts his girl in the family way. Hats off to the cock pheasant who does it without so much as a with your leave or by your leave. And no sooner done than the whole subject's off his mind.'

My eyes were now wet and stinging.

'It isn't true that my dad gave Ellen a baby and that her father sued him, though that's what ...'

'When I was about your age, I had a schoolfellow who told me how it works. "You know those two balls you have," he said. "Well, somehow one of them gets up into the woman's body, and then it grows into a baby. Then it comes out through her belly button." We used to play doctor. I remember getting a faint but definitely pleasant thrill from holding a toy trumpet against a little girl's belly. Her name was Wendy. I reckon my love for her was a far more worshipping kind of love than I have ever felt for anyone since. She was at the convent school.'

'Oh,' I whispered.

'But you want to talk about your dad?'

'I just wanted to explain that – '

'We all expect too much from our parents. You see. My own mother was a frivolous sort of person, not interested in anything beyond keeping up appearances. Red-and-white curtains – perhaps I mentioned that. Dogs on the lawn. My father never said "Well done" to me – not once. He used to smoke Abdulla cigarettes, the ones with the Egyptian soldiers on the packets. He was happiest in the barber's shop, that rich, boozy smell of bay rum and Latakia. But to me he was just a gruff-voiced elderly man forever saying "Don't".'

Abruptly Mr Blair heaved himself up, the fag-end in his mouth, pocketed his roller and shag, and strode out into the dark, crossing the yard to the shed which had once been used for incubators. There on the smooth wooden floor traces of his chalked-out plan for a new windmill could still be found, despite the defacement inflicted by Tom Frederick's piss. I found Mr Blair studying them by a weak electric light bulb while slowly rolling another fag.

'This windmill may be utopian,' he murmured.

'What's that, sir?'

'Utopia means nowhere,' he said. 'Never-never land, the Sugarcandy Mountain, imaginary windmills.'

It was then that I heard the sound of an engine in the yard and I shot outside, expecting to find another of our uninvited land surveyors and estate agents, or the man-in-the-new-hat, but what I saw was a large van parked beside the stables where old Boxer and Clover were sleeping out the winter on empty stomachs, their ribs showing through their hides. You couldn't see the lettering on the van but I knew it by heart:

'Alfred Simmonds, Horse Slaughterer and Glue Boiler, Porterstone. Dealer in Hides and Bone-Meal. Kennels Supplied.'

Old 'Knacker' Simmonds's boy, Sid, who was several years older than the rest of us, had turned 'friendly' soon after they took my father from Porterstone General Hospital up to London for tests. (Mum told me that dad had contracted some rare form of swine disease from the pigs; apparently it races to the brain and there's no cure.) Anyway, here he was, a grinning, affable Sid Simmonds with his dad, standing beside their smartly painted van, eyeing our two cart-horses by the light of oil lamps.

'Evening, Alex,' Sid called. I saw his shifty eyes swivel sharply as Mr Blair came out of the 'windmill' shed behind me. Mr Blair walked across to the van in his old tweed jacket with leather elbow patches and a fag-end in his mouth. Knacker Simmonds lifted his bowler hat.

'You must be the gentleman, sir,' Knacker said. 'Heard all about you.'

'Take a word of advice, Alex,' Sid said, 'that Boxer of yourn has that bad of a sore on his foreleg he won't be lasting much longer. No way of saving him with no hands on the farm.'

'Put the old boy out of his misery before he loses more

weight,' Knacker Simmonds added, addressing himself to Mr Blair.

I had in fact left a message for Hinchcliffe, our usual vet, but it was ten to one that Knacker had tipped him off we could no longer pay his fees.

I told Sid Simmonds to get lost. I must have been some sight: filthy, muck-ridden from head to toe, unwashed for days, my short trousers torn, my pullover in shreds, my hair matted, my eyes red from lack of sleep. But Mr Blair knew how to lift his shooting stick and how to sit on it. He insisted that Boxer's sore could be cured.

'I don't rightly know if you're familiar with current circumstances on this farm, sir,' Knacker grumbled.

'No money, you mean?'

'No farmer, no hired hands, no nothin', sir.'

'I shall visit Mr Hinchcliffe and settle his fee.'

I was impressed by Mr Blair's 'shall' and 'settle' and no longer had any doubt he'd been at Eton.

'Too much kindness killed the cat,' said Sid, adding, 'I reckon,' as if the thought was new to the world.

'My advice to you,' Mr Blair addressed Knacker, 'is to conduct your business by daylight.'

'Well, knock me down,' Knacker bridled, 'there's no doin' some folk a kindness. Begging your pardons, gentlemen.'

And off they went. Afterwards Knacker and Sid went around the village complaining about 'meddling strangers and spies'. Mr Blair likened Knacker to 'the sort of cock-sparrow type who'd be a sergeant-major only they aren't tall enough.'

It's odd to think that this incident, with our breath steaming from the February frosts, was to become, strangely transformed, one of the most famous passages in English literature, at least so I'm told by the authorities. Many years later I found the following passage in a literary encyclopaedia:

> Ask any youngster what he or she best remembers in the book, which scene most captured their imagination, and you will almost certainly hear, 'Poor old Boxer!' – Boxer lured inside Simmonds' van by Napoleon, believing it to be an ambulance, his great hoofs hammering in alarm when the awful truth dawns, and his gallant mate Clover galloping after him until her breath runs out. This scene draws its power not merely from our instinct for justice and fair-play, but from the simple truthfulness of the story-telling.

Truthfulness? I must leave that to greater minds than mine. I'd simply add, for the record, a word about Clover. That faithful mare continued throughout our confrontation to bend her white-striped nose over her meagre hay ration while Boxer's fate hung in the balance. Not a hoof moved, not an ear twitched.

Mr Blair fetched Hinchcliffe the following day, 'settled' his bill, and Boxer's sore later healed up. It was the first time that Mr Blair had spent the night on the farm.

'Shouldn't you go back to your mother for the night?' he asked.

'She knows where I am, sir.'

I think he suffered cruelly from the cold but he stayed with me for three days until we were through the worst of the lambing. I remember sleeping for twelve hours and waking to find him skinning a dead lamb to encourage the ewe to adopt an orphaned one. He had fettered the reluctant foster-mother's head to the stall, so that she couldn't see the wrong lamb reaching for her teats, but she was kicking it aside while her own lambs grew fatter.

'She's got ideas.' Mr Blair winked to cheer me up.

Though himself exhausted and coughing badly, he sat patiently prodding a rubber teat into the failing lamb's mouth, but it died in his arms. We fed her to Napoleon and Snowball.

Then Mr Blair had to leave. He had work to do – a book to write.

'You were away a long time last time,' I said, avoiding his eye.

He smiled at me gently. 'Blame a man called Eliot,' he said.

'Who's that, sir?'

'Alex, perhaps it's time for you and me to stop calling each other sir.'

'"Each other", sir?'

'There's a variety of humour called wit. You get some of it in Shakespeare, a great deal with the Restoration dramatists, and if you want to look closer to home, we have Wilde. Oscar Wilde.'

'Why, sir?'

'The importance of being earnest is wit.'

I stared at him.

'E-a-r-nest. E-r-nest. You see.'

I didn't. But Mr Blair's patience never ran out. And he hadn't lost sight of my question (even if I had):

'Who's Eliot? you ask. He's a very gifted poet and also one of the few Tories I can respect. He once turned down a book of mine, the one about the tramps, but I don't hold it against him. I persuaded him to read some of his poems on the radio, you see, to the Indians who aren't listening anyway. But there were hitches.'

'Will you be seeing him again?' I asked sulkily. 'Will there be more "hitches"?'

Mr Blair leaned on his shooting stick thoughtfully.

'I invited him to dinner at Mortimer Crescent last January. I wrote advising him to take the number 53 bus or get off the tube at Kilburn Park. Eileen and I cooked a special meal but he didn't turn up. I might send him the book I've been writing. When I've finished it. I still haven't got it right, you see.'

'The one with the talking pigs, si—'

'Yes, that one. Call me George.'

'George?'

'I told you why I don't like Eric. Most of my friends call me George so you'll just have to lump it.' We had reached the five-barred gate. 'There's a river in Suffolk called the Orwell,' he said. 'It snakes along the southern boundary of the county and reaches the sea thirty-five miles down the coast from Southwold. That's where my parents were living when I wrote my first book – the first one that got published. The tramps one.'

'So what about this Orwell river, then?'

He ignored my question.

'I always had the lonely child's gift of making up stories,' he said. 'I dare say I was getting my own back for my failure to meet the standards. You don't have to make up stories, Alex, because you're in the middle of one.'

I asked him what he meant. I wanted to know and I wanted to detain him, but he didn't answer. It was after dark and he glanced up towards the farmhouse with those eyes of his.

'There's light coming through the curtain,' he said. 'When

the war's over they'll keep us blacked out. They'll never allow us to show lighted windows again.'

'Why, sir?'

'George. Because every power they acquire they keep. They'll tell us we can throw away our ration cards but I shall hang on to mine. It will be a trick, you see. So long, Alex. Next Saturday, then?'

He strode away, turning just once to wave his shooting stick. I could hear his boots on the road long after I could see him.

I went up to the house and fiddled with the curtains, but I was thinking about the pennies on his dead father's eyes. There was something about Mr Blair himself which made you imagine him dead. This thought made me snivel a bit. Twenty years later, when I was negotiating the sale of lambs to France for fattening, a French colleague took me to see Chartres Cathedral 'en route' to one of those incredible, five-course lunches only the French can do. Looking up at the lean, ascetic saints and apostles carved and weathered on the façade, I recognised Mr Blair in all of them.

At that time I'd begun reading his earlier novels:

Your verminous Christian saints are the biggest hedonists of all. They're out for an eternity of bliss, whereas we poor sinners don't hope for more than a few years of it.

CHAPTER VII

Mr Blair was as good as his word and showed up at the farm the following Saturday but as soon as I caught sight of that long stride I didn't see any way to call him George because his name was Eric. I'd only lost two lambs throughout the week and I hoped he would pay for Hinchcliffe to come and look at three sick ones. But Mr Blair's mood on arrival was short-tempered and sullen. I thought he must be fed up with me and my starving animals – it was only later that he explained that he'd been suffering from something worse than a bullet in the throat, or shooting the elephant: he called it 'writer's block'.

He went straight for the big boars in their sties. At his approach Napoleon and Snowball began beating their weight against the boards, clamouring for swill. Mr Blair glowered at them suspiciously, as if he'd been quarrelling with them all week.

'Maybe Trotsky was a fraudulent utopian,' he said.

'Who's that, sir?'

'Who's Trotsky? He's Snowball with Napoleon's ice-axe in his skull.'

I couldn't think of anything to say, though I could imagine

Joe Pilkington and Tom Frederick sniggering.

I said: 'My dad always put the pigs first because they're the best money-earners.'

Mr Blair nodded: 'So the pigs are stuffing themselves, and starving the other animals – for the benefit of the other animals.'

'Well ... not exactly. But there's no offal left.'

'Two large boars are carrying the burden of what Rousseau called "the greatest good of the greatest number". And they know it, Napoleon and Snowball – don't they?'

I was probably close to tears. He led me into the house, collected my dad's spare shotgun, and told me to boil a kettle. Through the kitchen window I watched him striding towards the long pasture. I heard a shot, then another, and presently he reappeared dragging a dead ewe with great difficulty, very pale and wheezing. I ran out into the yard, horrified: this was the lambing season! But he brushed aside my wails and set about gutting the still-warm ewe.

'First things first,' was all he said.

Finally, having fed the ewe to Napoleon and Snowball – head, entrails, kidneys, liver – he came into the house, poured some hot water from the kettle into a tub, and washed his hands. He had a mania for washing – you may remember him calling 'a bath a day for everyone' true socialism. Now he settled down in my dad's Windsor chair to his strong tea, but his mood remained restless, even resentful.

'Alex,' he said, 'an intellectual is a person who cannot tell the bad from the worse.'

He must have meant me complaining about his shooting the ewe.

'What's inter— ... ?'

He reached into his pocket for his tobacco.

'An English intellectual would feel more ashamed of standing to attention during "God Save the King" than of stealing from a poor box.'

'I never did that!'

He was rolling his fag. 'An intellectual is a two-faced sodomite who'll always use a foreign word when a perfectly sound English one is available.'

'I don't know any foreign words!'

I expect my voice was high enough to crack a window. I was trembling. It may have been the ewe but I also felt that Mr Blair was playing unfair today, using his knowledge and long words to put me down. He seemed to be seething inside himself.

Without a word he got up and went out of the house. There was no sign of him in the main yard but I could just about catch wind of his reedy voice coming from the sties. I followed him on tiptoe, like stalking an enemy, which was how I felt. I found him leaning over the sties, addressing old Major, who was fast asleep:

'Asleep are you? Dreaming your dream? So what do we call you: Marx or Lenin? If Marx, where's Lenin in all this?'

Mr Blair was now leaning over Snowball: 'So where's Lenin round here? I'm looking for Lenin.'

Now it was Napoleon: 'You're no Lenin, are you? You'll suppress his testament, more likely. And end up in Jones's bed, eh?'

Back to old Major: 'You overlooked one thing: power.'

Snowball again: 'And after Kronstadt? What then?'

Now he moved across to the small, frisky porker Squealer, whose tail was tying itself in knots of excitement:

'Don't imagine that for years on end you can make yourself the boot-licking propagandist of the Soviet regime or any other regime, and then suddenly return to mental decency! Once a whore, always a whore!'

Mr Blair still hadn't spotted me. I didn't mind him talking to the pigs, why should I, but now he was leaning over Snowball again and I couldn't believe my ears:

'You don't want Jones back, do you? What use is a drunk on two legs to you? You don't want the tyranny of man, do you? And remember, comrade, your resolution must never falter. All men are enemies. All animals are comrades.'

Mr Blair looked up and saw me. The wildest rage and sense of betrayal overcame me. I picked up a stone and hurled it at him, aiming for his head – though probably I still had enough sense to make it a near-miss.

'Get out!' I yelled and picked up a larger stone, but he was on me, his long arms pinning mine.

'I wasn't talking about your father, Alex ... After all, Jones is a common enough name ... Isn't it?'

'Not on this farm! Talk about two-faced!'

'It's all just an idea, you see.'

'My dad isn't an idea! My dad isn't a drunk!'

Mr Blair set himself to chopping firewood, coughing badly from the effort. I could tell he was unhappy with what he'd done. We didn't talk for a while. When he took his handkerchief from his mouth I saw flecks of blood on it.

'You're still not calling me George,' he grumbled.

'I prefer Eric.'

'Well, it's *my* name, isn't it?'

'You changed Snowman's name to Snowball, and Charles's to Charlatan, and you called our stream the Irrawaddy and –'

He almost smiled, his mood eased. 'You're right. The dictatorship of the pigs will be a dictatorship of words ... in essence. The Seven Commandments. Words, words – ideas! Hm.'

'What Seven Commandments?'

'That's what's been holding me up all week. I can think of only four. Want to hear?'

I nodded sullenly.

'"Whatever goes upon two legs is an enemy. Whatever goes upon four legs, or has wings, is a friend. No animal shall kill any other animal. All animals are equal."'

'That's daft,' I said. 'Not killing other animals. You just killed a ewe to feed it to the pigs.'

'But I'm a man, you see. I think and behave like a man.'

'Someone's got to. And how can all animals be equal?'

'Like all men are equal.'

'Who says they are?'

'They should be.'

'I reckon some men are more "equal" than others.'

Mr Blair stared at me, his thin mouth slightly open, whereas he normally kept his lips in a single line.

'Say that again,' he said.

'Say what again?'

'About "equal".'

I shrugged. 'Can't remember.'

'Yes you can. You must. Say it again.'

'I reckon some men are more "equal" than others.'

He snapped his long fingers. 'That's it,' he said. 'That's it.'

'That's what?'

'That's it. That's the line. That's it. That's the line I've been looking for.'

'What line, then?'

'Your line: "All animals are equal but some animals are more equal than others."'

'I never said that.'

'Yes you did.'

'I never.'

'Hm. I need three more commandments. What about "No animal shall sleep in a bed"?'

'A bed?'

'A human bed.'

I chortled.

'What about "No animal shall wear clothes"?'

'Clothes!'

'What about "No animal shall drink alcohol"?'

I laughed a lot at that. 'Eric, you're bonkers.'

'Hm. Think of something better. Something as good as your "more equal than others".'

'What's so amazing about that, anyway?'

' "More equal" – brilliant – don't you understand?'

'No.'

Presently he led me back into the farmhouse. From his canvas haversack he now produced a Lyons cake with pink icing, or half a cake, wrapped in old newspaper. He carefully cut it into two unequal portions, and invited me to choose. I was hungry. There had been times when I showed up in Porterstone, famished.

'Just walks in! Expecting a three-course dinner!'

I chose the smaller portion. Mr Blair stilled my hand.

'The big bit's yours,' he said. 'An intellectual would have chosen the fatter one. Their socialism is all on paper, you see. In other words, fruit-juice drinkers, nudists, sandal-wearers, Quakers, Nature Cure quacks, pacifists and feminists. The nancy boys and the pansies.'

'I don't understand that kind of stuff,' I said. 'And I don't want you ever to talk to the pigs like you did – Eric.'

'Eric still! And I gave you the bigger slice of cake!' He seemed in a better mood now. 'So how's your mother doing in Willingdon?' he asked.

'Willingdon? We live in Porterstone.'

His eyes flickered downright shiftily. 'Ah yes ...'

'You can change a pig's name, Eric, but not a village's.'

'You think? I'm not inclined to allow other literary gents to retrace the outsize prints of my boots in your mud. You now live in Willingdon, young man. So does Knacker Simmonds.'

We sat in a comfortable silence.

'Like to hear a good story?' he asked. I nodded. 'It's by Jack London,' he said. '"Love of Life." A gold prospector somewhere in the frozen wastes of Canada is struggling desperately towards the sea, dying of starvation but kept going by force of will. A wolf, also dying of hunger and disease, is creeping after him, waiting for the man to grow too weak to resist attack. By the time they come within sight of the sea both man and beast are crawling on their bellies. But the man's will is stronger – it is he who eats the wolf.'

Mr Blair glanced at his watch; I could tell that he'd grown weary of the story-telling as soon as he'd started and had boiled it all down to a few lines. He rolled himself another fag.

'How does the man kill the wolf?' I asked.

'That wolf has been following me all week,' he said.

'You?'

'Either the story eats the writer or the writer eats the story. Shall I tell you about my wife Eileen?'

I shrugged. 'It's up to you.'

A pained expression crossed his face.

'She read English at Oxford and when I met her she was studying again.'

'Why did she have to go to Oxford to read English? You can do that anywhere.'

'To "read" a subject at a university means to study it. Anyway, Eileen gave it all up to live in a village and look after me and the goats. We had a shop called The Stores. You'd be lying in on a Sunday morning when someone would bang on the door wanting a mousetrap. Eileen's brother Laurence was a Fellow of the Royal College of Surgeons. He looked after me when I was bedridden for most of six months. After that they sent me to Morocco and Eileen came along. Finally I told her I was attracted to the Arab girls – she agreed that I could have one of them, just once. She's not easily shocked, you see.'

Mr Blair had said all this in his dreariest voice – he made even the Arab girl sound like a piece of cheddar from his village store. I sensed that he was telling me all this out of some sense of duty, but I couldn't fathom what it was.

'When the war began Eileen moved to London to work in propaganda and I stayed with the village store and writing a few things. But then she lost her brother – she loved him very much, you see. He was killed at Dunkirk – mortally wounded in the chest by shrapnel while studying chest wounds in a field hospital. Eileen used to send me to Waterloo station to meet the troops and try to pick up news of him. It knocked the spirit out of Eileen, Laurence's death. She barely spoke for months and the seams in her stockings weren't straight. But she's more herself now, you see ... though it seems we aren't going to have any children.'

I waited.

'Eileen sends you her ... this cake we've eaten. She says

next time she'll bake the cake herself. I've told her all about you.'

'About me?'

'She'd like to meet you.'

'How?'

'Maybe she could come down one weekend.'

'She wouldn't like it here,' I said quickly. 'Not a lady, here.'

He registered my reaction, nodded and stood up. 'Time to go,' he said.

'I bet you were never in Burma and never shot an elephant,' I said quickly.

'I was never in Burma, as you rightly say, but I did shoot the elephant – in Clapham High Street, from the top deck of the omnibus.'

'Rubbish! I bet you were never a tramp either!'

'I did it for a week but travelled by Rolls Royce and dined every night at the Ritz. You've got me again.'

'And I bet you were never down a mine in Wigan!'

'Where are the handcuffs?'

But then he looked at his watch again and I felt a pull in my stomach.

'Must go, Alex,' he murmured.

Five minutes later we were standing at the five-barred gate. His hand touched mine. 'I don't like to leave you alone on the farm after dark, Alex.'

Suddenly I remembered Hinchcliffe. 'We need that vet again,' I said.

'How much will he charge?'

'Seven and six . . . probably.'

'Tell him I'll pay him on my next visit.'

'He won't believe me.'

Mr Blair fished in his jacket pockets and counted out the

money into my grubby hand. Then he found an extra florin.

'For you,' he muttered.

'That's too much,' I said.

'Is it? I'll take it back, then.'

After a moment I gave it back to him. He had big hands. I watched the gleaming silver coin vanish into his pocket. He pulled out his wallet and gave me a brown ten-shilling note, five times as much, more money than I'd ever had in my life, and I wondered whether this meant he was never coming back.

'Why don't we go for a slap-up tea to the Crown Hotel next time?' he said.

'Gosh! Mean it?'

'Mean it.'

'When?'

'Next time.'

'But when?'

'Soon. I'm ... I'm having work problems.'

'Is it that Eliot man again?'

'No. But it soon may be. So long.'

'So long, Eric.'

'George.'

He waited for me to say George but I wouldn't and off he strode. As usual he paused just once, to wave his stick – and soon there was only the echo of his boots on the road. After a while you'd hear nothing but if you waited you'd catch the sound again, fainter.

I received a second visit from Fred, the German-Jew spy who'd been kidnapped by Napoleon, and his Lagonda. He smelt of some fancy shaving cream and you could tell he'd oiled his straight-back hair with jasmine or something. He greeted me as if we'd been pals all our lives. I took him into the house this time, because he'd brought me a big box of chocolates, but when I invited him to sit down he couldn't help dusting the chair with his calf-skin gloves.

'So how's George's book?' he asked as casually as if inquiring about the next full moon.

'Dunno, sir. He doesn't talk about it.'

Fred's mood darkened and his jaw set. 'Did you tell George I was here?'

'Oh, no, sir. Give us a ride in the car, sir.'

The large nose which grew straight out of Fred's forehead gave me a kind of sundial reading.

'Did George ever tell you about his schooldays?'

'He was at Eton, sir,' I said proudly. 'And you were at Westminster Abbey.'

'So you did tell him I was here?'

I went red. 'Yes, sir. He's my friend, sir.'

'And I'm not?'

'Well ...'

'Didn't I give you ten shillings?'

'One shilling!'

'Not enough, eh? George gives you more, is that it?' He regarded me with trembling anger, then looked about our living-room with disgust. 'So this is the dilapidated film-set where George will bury socialism by praising it?'

My own temper was rising.

'I didn't ask you for money, did I? I suppose you think that you can ponce down here in your posh car and buy anything on two legs?'

'I assume you're quoting George,' Fred said.

'Eric says all publishers are swindlers.'

I thought Fred was going to cry. But then he stood up like a Great War officer.

'How about a ride in my car? Show you some acceleration.'

I wiped my nose on my sleeve. I wasn't quite done with him.

'I might get the seat dirty, mightn't I?'

Fred drove like a madman along the narrow, winding road between the farm and Porterstone, stopped to buy me five bags of potato crisps, then roared off up the main road to London while my eyes were glued to the speedometer and the rev counter and all the other dazzling dials set in circular silver frames in the real-wood dashboard.

Fred said: 'George is a Puritan. That's his strength and his failing. As a boy he always believed he smelt and was ugly. He dresses to suit himself but there's always a recent bath underneath. *Mens sana in corpore sano* – that's very middle-class. At Eton he used to advise his friends to stop wasting their time on Virgil and to read Shaw, Wells, Wilde and Swift. Expose the swindles. He's like a Thames barge slowly horning through the fog. "Of course," he says, "Shaw doesn't care what kind of dictatorship we have in England because he isn't English, is he?" '

Fred used his own horn a lot and more or less blasted anything slow-moving off the road until we came to a herd of Jersey cows.

'Slow down,' I commanded. 'You'll scare them. They're in calf.'

Fred obeyed. Well, he had to. The mud-caked flanks of the cows began knocking against the gleaming wings of the Lagonda. I was thinking of offering to wash it down afterwards for a shilling.

Fred plucked a Turkish cigarette from his fancy case and fitted it into his ivory holder.

'Shall I tell you about George's prep school?' he said as if offering me a box of Aladdin's Turkish Delight.

'He wet his bed. A lady almost thrashed him with her riding crop and he had to call the headmaster's wife "Mum". He told me.'

Fred looked disappointed.

'He was brilliant!' he declared, as if I'd been insisting that Eric was some kind of half-wit. 'He won a scholarship to Eton, fourteenth in his Election. But he never bothered much with his Greek and Latin. You couldn't compare him to the great scholars of his Election – Sir Steven Runciman, the historian of Byzantium and the Crusades, Sir Roger Mynors, Professor of Latin at Oxford. So it was Burma for George. A friend of mine had dinner with him in Rangoon. At that time he was the very model of an Empire builder, intolerant of any native who made a nuisance of himself. Punishments and beatings were all they understood. He used the magazine *Adelphi* for target practice and called it a "scurrilous rag".'

'Probably was,' I said cheerfully. The cows were still rubbing the shine off Fred's Lagonda. He kept glancing at his gold watch.

'Did he tell you about his time as a tramp?' he asked.

'He was a plawnjeer.'

'That was Gollancz's book, of course. Not a patch on *Catalonia* – which was my book. He offered Gollancz four pen-names because he didn't want his family to find out what he'd been doing in Paris. When I first met him I thought he was a queer cove. You'd find him sitting in some bar or café, all by himself, looking like death, and then he'd stride off, huddled in his threadbare coat, to his bug-infested room, where he'd hit his typewriter far into the night.'

'Was he writing?'

Fred was about to ruffle my matted hair, which I didn't care for, but he thought better of it, probably on behalf of his fancy gloves.

'He's probably a genius, Alex. Your friend Eric. But don't expect any recognition or gratitude.'

'What for?'

'The people who helped George when he went north to Wigan never received a free copy or any thanks at all. And of course *Gollancz* was too busy admiring Stalin to send free copies to humble people who didn't happen to be famous reviewers.'

'What's a reviewer?'

We were through the cows now. Fred revved the engine under its long super-bonnet. The acceleration was fantastic. My eyes were glued to the dials. I longed to get behind the wheel. My dad had let me have a go with the Ford, when we had it.

'Alex,' Fred sighed, 'I must acquire the rights to this book.'

'Hm.'

'I know he's almost finished it! I ran into him by chance some months ago. He said he was trying to write a little story – "just a squib," he said – about animals, but it wasn't working out. He was wrapped in gloom. He told me he'd found a semi-abandoned farm but he wouldn't say where.'

I was studying the dials on the dashboard. We'd hit ninety.

'George said the adults had left the farm but a wild boy, a kind of wolf-boy, a Mowgli out of Kipling, was refusing to budge. George found you so fascinating that he kept wanting to write about you, rather than the animals.'

I thought about this.

'Eric never said I was an Indian. And you're a liar.'

'Just a humble publisher.'

I thought about that, too. On the radio and in comics foreign spies called themselves 'humble' in oily voices: 'Your humble servant, Mr Hannay.'

'Why won't he show me the book, Alex?'

'Dunno.'

'Who can understand a genius capable of writing two letters to the same man in a single day, each with a different signature? A writer who had two different names sign-written on his office door at the BBC?'

Fred was now heading back for Porterstone, driving with one hand as usual.

'How long is the pig-book, Alex?'

'I dunno!'

'He must have read some chapters to you.'

'No, sir!'

'Call me Fred. Just the first few pages, perhaps? How does it begin?'

'Honest!'

'He told you not to tell me?'

'Eric's never told me what I should say about anything.'

Fred dropped me off in Porterstone, the car park of the Crown Hotel, where he was obviously planning to treat himself to a spiv's dinner, leaving me to hoof it back to the farm. It was obvious that Fred had given up on me and there was no shilling this time.

CHAPTER VIII

The daffodils were out, I remember, and the forsythia, the season of singing birds, but no spring shoots were pushing through the neglected fields of Manor Farm. Pilkington turned up with Joe and two dogs to collect my sickly lambs, waving a piece of paper bearing my mother's signature. Then the whole flock went. The red dye on their fleeces was sheared off and replaced by Pilkington's blue dye as the kicking beasts were loaded into his van. He told me to help. I sat on a log and lighted a cigarette. Pilkington called me a juvenile delinquent and warned me I'd end up in the Borstal. Joe's superior smirk as he collared the sheep cornered by his dogs sealed his fate thirty years later – I am patient.

I flew into Porterstone on two wheels. My mum was in school, helping with the dinners, shaming me. I hung around in the grotty, damp room above the shop to escape Ma Pyke's complaints. I poked about among bills and letters from 'solicitors' which I didn't understand, though you could tell they were unfriendly. 'Dear Madam, I beg to inform you that unless ... unless this, unless that ... within a week ... we have been instructed by our clients ... we shall be constrained to ...'

I might have felt pity for her but in my heart, I suppose, I blamed her for what had happened between my dad and Ellen. The things Mr Blair had said to me about married women letting themselves go had sunk in. It was true: I couldn't remember a time when my mum had spoken of, or to, my dad without a kind of scorn, as if anything he did was wrong. Or crude, stupid, uneducated. So I reckoned she'd driven him to it – to Ellen, I mean. And Pilkington had just walked off with our entire flock.

My mum no sooner came upstairs from the shop than I flew into a rage about the sheep.

'What did he pay you, eh?'

'You shut your mouth, Alex. What do you know about animal prices?'

'I know Pilkington robbed us. And who fed those lambs? Who kept them alive? And where's my dad?' I yelled. 'What have you done with him?'

She sat on the bed, her hands meekly folded in her lap.

'Maybe you'll know one day,' she murmured. 'That school inspector is threatening me with the court if you don't mend your ways.'

'That sod.'

'Enough of that language! They're accusing you of vandalism, my boy.'

'Like what?'

'Like breaking school windows at night, that's what! Like cutting hedges and fences round Pinchfield and Foxwood, that's what!'

'I never!'

'And slashing Pilkington's tyres when he was parked behind the Crown one night – that's what!'

'Prove it!'

She said: 'I'll make you some supper, Alex. I've got some fresh eggs for you. You'll stop growing if you don't look out.'

I cycled back to the farm on a full stomach, plotting further actions against the Pilkingtons. But then my mind turned to Mr Blair – I wanted to talk to Eric. Sullenly I counted the days he'd been away.

Two days later he showed up. I hid my tears of joy and rage in the barn. I could hear him tramping about, taking in the situation, then he started talking to the pigs again.

'So which of you is Lenin? Who sabotaged the windmill? Who signed the Nazi–Soviet Pact?'

After a long while he called my name, wheezing. Finally I slunk out of the barn into the daylight, a filthy, ragged urchin who hadn't washed or changed his clothes in weeks. But Mr Blair nodded as if we'd been apart barely a day.

'The songs and smells of early summer mingling and ascending like the smoke of ever-burning altars,' he said. 'I took the early train. In a field near the railway line I saw a month-old calf, flat as a Noah's Ark animal, bounding stiff-legged after its mother.'

'No calves here,' I muttered. 'No sheep either.' I had a bad cold and my nose and throat were clogged with snot. There was dried snot on my hands and sleeves, too.

'Did Pilkington take the sheep?'

'Fat lot you care. You and "Lenin".'

Eric turned to lay a hand on my matted hair but I stepped away.

'Tea at the Crown Hotel, Alex!'

'What?'

I didn't really want to go. I did and I didn't. I'd never been in the Crown. It wasn't for our sort.

Eric said: 'Get some of that dirt off your hands, face, neck and knees, and off we go.' From his haversack he unwrapped a brand-new shirt and a pair of short grey trousers. 'Try them for size,' he said. 'They're from Eileen.'

He had brought his bicycle on the train, a Triumph from the time of King Charles I by the look of it, I've never seen one like it. So we cycled into Porterstone and Eric told me one story after another, mainly war stories, as if to prevent me from turning back.

'During the First World War the army needed horses,' Eric wheezed, struggling for breath as he pedalled. 'I once saw a cabman burst into tears in the market place when they took his horse from him.' We pedalled on. 'All wars are about margarine,' he added.

THE CROWN HOTEL. Open to Non-residents. LUNCHEONS–TEAS–DINNERS. DANCE HALL AND TENNIS COURTS. Parties catered for.

We stowed our bikes in the yard behind the hotel and in we went. I'd walked past the Crown all my life but never given it a glance. There was a kind of expensive smell in the hallway. Eric chuckled:

'Dead flowers, chintz and the rinsings of wine bottles.'

I saw a brick fireplace with inglenooks, beams across the ceiling, oak panelling, gate-leg tables, a hammered iron chandelier and pewter plates hanging on the wall. There were hunting prints and stags' heads and posh carpets. But I doubt I saw any of it, I wasn't looking, I was too scared-stiff, it all comes from Eric's novels. It's not the Crown I'm describing but all of his terrible hotels rolled into one. I did smell lavender furniture polish. You could have heard a pin drop.

After quite some time this stuck-up old waiter in a black

coat and winged collar stepped out of the shadows and took a long look at us.

Eric said: 'Tea for two.'

The old waiter hesitated. Eric was scarcely the Aga Khan in his baggy cords and old jacket, and with a dead fag-end in his mouth.

'Your scones are fresh, I hope,' Eric said.

Without a word the old snob led us to a table in the darkest corner of the dining-room but Eric said, 'We'll sit over there by the window.'

So we sat by the window and Eric told the waiter, 'Make sure they scald the tea pot. We want Indian tea, very strong, no sugar.'

'Yes, sir.' Or did he say 'sare'? Did he say, 'Tea, sare? Yes, sare? Zees way.'? No, I think that one was in Eric's novel about aspidistras.

Eric nodded in dismissal, then leaned his leather elbow patches on the tablecloth and predicted 'little wilting sandwiches and rock cakes like balls of putty at two shillings a head.' He told me how he'd once taken a lady friend – not Eileen, he added – out to eat a set tea in a posh hotel and he'd got 'caught out' by the price of it, with the result that he'd had to borrow his bus fare home from the lady.

'How can you make love when you have only eightpence left? Then afterwards she slips half a crown and twenty Gold Flake into your pocket.' He smiled his gaunt smile. 'That was worse than getting shot in the neck.' My mouth must have hung open. 'Mind you, the two incidents had one thing in common,' he added.

'What?'

'Served me right on both occasions.'

'Are you sure you've got enough money?' I whispered.

'The lord of all, the money-god
Who rules us blood and hand and brain,
Who gives the roof that stops the wind,
And, giving, takes away again.'

He tapped the panelled wall behind his chair. 'Not even wood,' he said, 'another fake.' Then he told me that in Germany food rationing applied to meals eaten out as well as food you bought and took home. He winked: 'So that's why we're bound to win.'

The tea didn't arrive so he told me he'd once seen a man hanged in Burma. A few yards from the rope the condemned prisoner had stepped aside to avoid a puddle.

'Why?'

'He knew he was going to die but he didn't really believe it.'

'He might have wanted to swing with dry feet.'

The tea arrived. Eric immediately lifted the lid of the pot and peered inside. Then he grunted, indicating 'not good but not so bad either.'

'Tuck in,' he commanded.

'Are you sure you've got any money?' I asked.

'We'll think about that later,' he said. 'In Spain I once got a Fascist soldier in my sights but I couldn't pull the trigger. Know why?'

'Why?'

'Because he was holding up his trousers as he ran.'

I thought about this. 'His braces must have snapped.'

'He'd been relieving himself. He'd gone to the bog.'

'Why do you write, Eric? I hate writing.'

'George still no good?'

I shook my head.

'Why do I write? It's always and unquestionably political. But I never sit down and say I'm going to write a work of art.'

'Why?'

'Why what?'

'Why don't you ... sit down?'

Eric leaned closer to me across the table. His thin moustache was stretched along his upper lip and his eyes were deep-sunk in their sockets.

'Because I don't flinch.'

I had now lost track of what he was saying, or I was asking, and my eye was fastened on the scones and currant cake which the old waiter had just laid before us. I'd spotted one real strawberry floating in the jam.

'Shall I tell you where Swift flinched?' Eric said. 'He flinched about sending Gulliver to the bog.'

'Sir?' (This lapse I attributed to the cake and jam.)

'Gulliver wakes up in captivity, doesn't he, bound head and foot. He's hungry – so they feed him. Meat and drink. And what do we all feel the need to do after eating and drinking?'

This seemed to be a question to ask after we'd tackled the scones and cake. I don't think it was exactly cruelty on Eric's part, just that he'd been a schoolmaster and had never shaken off the bad habits. I think schoolmasters believe that waiting for cake and jam is good for a boy's character, or something.

Now Eric's way of speaking changed; it seemed to belong to the bygone age of wigs and silver buckles I'd seen in the illustrated edition of *Gulliver* he'd given me for Christmas. I could tell at once he was imitating Gulliver but making it up:

'So urgent were my discomforts according to the promptings of nature that, having made some progress in learning their language, I was able to persuade his Majesty's scholars of the awkwardness of my condition, which was duly conveyed to the Emperor. His answer, when it came, and as I could apprehend it, was that this must be a work of time, not to be thought on without the advice of his council. Whereupon my bowels, like slaves driven beyond obedience by desperation, let out an enormous explosion of foul-smelling gas, the noise and odour of which caused all but his Majesty to fall to the ground. An imperial commission was then issued out, obliging all the villages to despatch ten thousand men to resolve my inconvenience by digging a vast pit at the farthest and remotest end of the island, this work to be undertaken by the humblest kind of citizen, including felons, convicts and those who had dared to question that the sun and the stars had been created by his Majesty in the course of a single night. Their work being done, I was permitted to unburden myself in gratifying solitude, even at the risk of my escape or worse mischief that I might inflict.'

I could see the old waiter listening intently in the shadows, hiding behind a palm in a pot.

'Did you make all that up?' I asked, though I knew the answer. Eric nodded. 'Does "odour" mean smell?' I asked. He nodded. 'Fred said you don't like smells. Do I smell, Eric – because of the farm?'

Eric smiled faintly and took himself to the gents – his Gulliver speech seemed to me a long-winded way of having a crap. Anyway, I could no longer stare at the cake. I cut it in two, then examined the halves, then took the smaller, with the old waiter's eye on me all the time.

Eric came back, eased his long stick-limbs into his chair, lighted a fag, and urged me to 'polish off' the remaining cake and the scones. He told me he'd recently broadcast an interview with Jonathan Swift on the radio.

'But he's dead!' I protested.

'I brought him back to life.' Eric flicked his long brown fingers. 'Just like that. He was wearing knee-breeches, a wig and a three-cornered hat. Well, he would, wouldn't he?'

I nodded.

'I showed Mr Swift my own edition of his work, lively woodcuts and crooked capital letters, printed between 1730 and 1740 in twelve small volumes, with calf covers but a bit the worse for wear. I complained to him that I found the long, old-fashioned 's's a nuisance – kept mistaking them for 'f's.'

'What did Mr Swift say about all that?'

'He seemed mainly interested in my leather elbow patches. Never seen anything like them on a gentleman, he said. He wanted to know whether everyone now wore elbow patches and printed 's's like snakes.'

'Really?'

Eric looked at me rather tenderly.

'How would you like to come and live with me in London?' he asked.

My mouth was crammed with scone.

'We'd get on, the two of us, don't you think?' he said. 'We haven't any children of our own, you see. Eileen works in the Ministry of Food,' he added.

'I thought you said she was in prop— ... prop— ...'

'Food is propaganda nowadays.'

'Does she get extra rations?'

'No. But we always have good roast beef and Yorkshire pudding on Sundays. Eileen makes the best pastry in London. You like roast beef, don't you?'

'Yes!'

'With the potatoes roasted under the joint so that the juices seep into them. And toad in the hole?'

I nodded. Somehow I couldn't look him in the eye.

'Why can't you have children of your own?' I asked.

'Because I've never had any.'

'Why?'

'I'm probably sterile.'

'What's sterile?'

'It's the one thing I have in common with Hitler.'

My mouth hung open. 'One ball, you mean?'

'I had two when I last counted. Maybe it's Eileen who's infertile, but I think it's me. There's no way of testing these things, you see.'

I was eating steadily.

'So we'd like to adopt a son,' Eric said. 'A boy of ten –'

'Twelve!'

'A boy of twelve called Alex.'

'What about my mum?'

He frowned slightly. 'Should I speak to her?'

I shook my head. 'She wouldn't want me in the Blitz.'

'It's quite safe,' he said. 'I always know when a doodle-bug's heading our way because I can feel Eileen's heart beating faster against me. From time to time you get bombed out and have to move, that's all.'

'You could come and live on our farm,' I said, 'with me and my mum – get things going again.'

'I can't leave Eileen alone, you see, and I can't afford to buy your farm, though I might after the book's finished.'

'Buy it? It's ours.'

He sighed. 'Alex, you won't be able to hang on without

income or capital. Not for ever. But if I can get some money out of those swindlers for this book, I could probably buy the farm, you see, for a fair price, and hire a couple of hands, and your mother could live there, and you could come down to see her and work on the farm at weekends.' He paused. 'Still skipping school, are you, Alex?'

The blood rushed to my face. He'd never mentioned this before, though Joe had very decently told him. Now it wasn't Eric sitting opposite me but the 'schoolmaster'.

'I take that silence to be a form of affirmation,' he said. 'Unless you go to school, Alex, you'll never know what words like "affirmation" mean. Unless you go to school, Alex, you may end up selling matches on the Thames Embankment. Or unemployed in Wigan. Or washing dishes in Paris. Or knocking on the doors of convents for a "cup o' tay". Unless you go to school, Alex, you'll never know how to manage your own farm. And you'll miss the best thing in life – which is what?'

I was staring at the floor.

'The best thing in life is the ability to share the thoughts of greater minds.'

I sort of nodded.

'What about the Porterstone Grammar School, Alex? Are they operating the eleven-plus entrance?'

I nodded.

'You're twelve, aren't you? Did you sit the exam?'

'They said my maths was OK but not my English.'

'Can you take it again?'

I nodded.

'But you've been doing a bunk. Of course some adolescents benefit by higher education, others do not. After ten or twelve you have to separate the more gifted children from the less gifted. But I think you're gifted. You'd prosper at the grammar school.'

'Can't afford it, my mum says. I did get a place, but not a free scholarship place.'

'Hm. They say they're going to make all grammar school places free under the new Education Act, but easier said than done and by the time they get round to it you'll be shaving.'

I shrugged.

'What you need is some tuition to get you through the Common Entrance.'

'What's that?'

'Of course it would depend on how well the book does and what I can afford ...'

'You mean a private school, one of those posh places you were talking about?'

'Not a posh one, but ... I've been working it out, you see. You'd have a father, two mothers, and your farm. It would be your farm because you'd be my adopted son.' He glanced at his watch, a gesture I knew well and always dreaded. 'We can go and talk to your mother now. You could take the train with me back to London. Just for a few days. To meet Eileen. She can probably wangle some new clothes for you.'

'What about the farm?'

'There's a general stock auction in Feltenham next Thursday. We can sell off your remaining livestock and re-stock the farm later. Napoleon and Snowball should fetch a fair price.'

'What about Boxer and Clover?'

'I spoke to Simmonds.'

'To Knacker!'

'It would break the bank to feed those two old horses back to full strength.'

I knew he was right, but I shook my head sullenly.

'The alternative,' he went on, 'is to sell the farm by auction and for you to begin a new life in London with me and Eileen.'

'What about my mum?'

'We could set her up in a small general store in the village: groceries, sweets, packets of aspirin, *Magnet* and *Gem*, kids' editions of *Treasure Island* and *Gulliver*, that sort of thing. In a grocer's shop people come in to buy things –'

'Mousetraps on Sunday mornings!'

'Whereas in a bookshop they come in to make a nuisance of themselves. In our store we used to sell about thirty shillings of merchandise a week. It covered the rent but your mother could do better than that. But I must talk to her, you see.'

I shook my head. All I knew was that I wanted to keep my mum and Eric separate: if ever Eric spoke to my mum the farm would be sold to Pilkington or Frederick. But I felt sure that the swindlers would pay Eric for his book, the one about talking pigs and looking for Lenin, then he could buy the farm, and adopt me, and the farm would still be mine, like he said, and he could come and see me at weekends, and my mum wouldn't mind because I would be living with her and not with this Eileen in London.

It all seemed quite clear and I was sorry that Eric looked so dejected and down in the mouth, even though I thanked him for the slap-up tea. When the bill came he fished in the pockets of his trousers and tweed jacket and just about found the necessary coins, with a tip. It was a close shave.

I watched him load his bike on to the train. I planned to cycle back to the farm. I didn't really expect to see him again. He sort of smiled faintly and waved a bit through the window as the engine worked up steam, but I felt he was wishing I'd take myself off and not just stand there. He looked quite heartbroken.

CHAPTER IX

The weeks passed but no sign of Eric. I couldn't forget the hollowed-out look on his face as his train had pulled out of Porterstone station. Our tea at the Crown Hotel kept going round in my head. I clung to the hope that Eric would come back and buy the farm, for me and my mum to live in, and then he would adopt me, and visit us every weekend (but not with his wife), and I'd inherit the farm from Eric in his will.

Constable Gill was standing like a blue lamp-post outside the door as I rode in from one of my night-time 'commando' raids. My mum had bought me a map of France with flagged stickers for the different armies after the D-Day landings. She let me take it back to my room in the farmhouse. There was a big battle going on around Caen, just as Eric had predicted, and I saw my raids on Pilkington as sorting out the Huns. But Constable Gill didn't.

He took my haversack off my back and slowly removed its contents: one castration knife; a hacksaw; a wire-cutter; a small axe; a bag of six-inch nails; a now-empty bottle smelling of paraffin; some cotton wadding-with-fuse; a box of matches I'd pilfered from Ma Pyke's shop.

'Well, Alex,' said Constable Gill, 'how do you explain all this?'

I didn't.

'Proper incendiary, aren't we?'

I saw no need to mention Mr Blair's gorilla-Home-Guard training. I offered Constable Gill a cup of tea. He said no, on his dignity.

'Aw, come on, Harry.'

'Who are you calling Harry?'

'My dad called you Harry.'

He weakened. I knew he liked lots of sugar in his tea (thank you again, Ma Pyke). He told me my 'antics' were a 'threat to the nation in time of war'.

'Aw.'

'Anyways, my boy, they're doing you no good and I'm here to read the Riot Act, see?'

'What's that, then, Harry?'

'Enough of your cheek.'

'More sugar in your tea?'

'They'll put you in the Borstal, my lad, and but for me you'd be there already. Lucky for you I always enjoyed a pint or two with Ron, your dad.'

'What did they do with my dad?' I asked. 'My mum won't tell me.'

'She didn't?'

I shook my head.

'Then it's not for me,' he said. He shuffled his big boots on the kitchen floor. 'You've had a hard time, Alex, a rotten time. I hate to see a good family come to grief like that.'

He wanted me to promise him I'd 'desist'.

'What's that, then?'

'No more antics, lad, that's what it is.'

I told him that Pilkington had stolen all our sheep.

'The sooner your mum sells this farm the better. Cut your losses, I say.'

'Where's my dad, Harry?'

'I'm not allowed to say.'

'No friend of his, you. No friend of mine, neither. I might burn down Pilkington's barn tonight.'

Constable Gill stood up. Then sat down. 'Alex, your dad's dead.'

'You're lying!'

'Am I? So where's his shotgun? They took it away with him, you see – coroner's inquest.'

So Joe had been right. Joe had known all along. They'd all known, everyone in Porterstone except me.

There was still no sign of Eric. About Easter-time, old Ted Hare died. My mum went to the funeral in the chapel. She said there was no one else who'd work a few hours for a few bob, like Ted. She didn't sound too down about it. I could tell she was about to sell the farm. I told her that if she kept the farm I knew how to get her a general store of her own, selling groceries, comics and aspirin.

'Whatever nonsense is that?' she said. 'Who's been filling your head? Is it that Mr Blair of yours?'

'He's got a plan to buy the farm for a fair price, you see.'

(I remember the 'you see', because I was trying to sound like Eric himself.)

'Oh he has, has he? He never thought of talking to *me* about it – and I know why.'

'Thing is, you see, he first needs to get the money from the swindlers.'

'Does he! So what kind of a swindler is your Mr Blair?'

I lost my temper. 'You don't understand anything. You're

just stupid. But for you my dad would never have done it!'

'Done what?' She was trembling.

'Done himself in.'

'Who told you that nonsense?'

Still no sign of Eric. More strangers in smart overcoats sniffing around the farm, measuring fields, prodding sick animals, tearing more strips of rotten wood from the sills. I knew Eric couldn't buy the farm until the swindlers had paid him for his book. Alone on the farm at night, I had a recurring dream of several swindlers with hats pulled over their eyes, all of them resembling Knacker Simmonds and Sid, pushing pound notes into Eric's hand in some filthy, gaslit alley in Lambeth. And cheating him. And Eric giving it all away to Bozo and the other tramps and pavement artists until there was no money left for buying our farm. I'd come out of the dream into a summer dawn, with the birds making their racket, and feel the stabbing hunger pains in my stomach. I'd taken to eating raw spuds and they weren't doing me any good. When I sicked-up in the sties, Napoleon had it down his snout before the others could move.

One Saturday in high summer I saw Eric's thick mop of hair moving between the hedgerows, his stick swiping at the cow parsley. It sounds silly, but my heart leapt and raced. I'd never been so pleased to see anyone. It was as good as if my dad had come back. I ran down to the five-barred gate to greet him.

'Eric! Eric!'

Eric was wearing gaiters. I saw at once that he was in a black mood.

'So what have you been up to?' he said.

Then he was stalking about the farm like an inspector

from the Ministry, muttering about 'dilapidation and noxious weeds'. With the sheep gone the pasture was an uncropped jungle, the ploughed field was a tangle of bindweed and couch grass, the plough was rusting in the open, Boxer and Clover lay panting in their stalls, too weak to haul it, and Eric's favourite pigs could barely offer him a grunt of greeting.

'This can't go on,' he said.

'I was waiting for you to get the money from the swindlers,' I muttered.

'You shouldn't believe everything I tell you,' he said.

I stared at him. His hard-set expression softened somewhat.

'Eileen and I were bombed out of our flat again, you see.'

'Was she killed?'

'She was at the Ministry, since you ask.'

'How's your book?' He didn't reply. 'Maybe you could go back to work for the BBC,' I said. 'To get the money.'

He strode back to the sties, where he prodded old Major, Napoleon, Snowball and Squealer with his stick, stirring none of them from their stinking, fly-infested torpor. And this, for some reason, suddenly set his temper blazing:

'Courtiers! Careerists! Arse-lickers! Toadies!'

His angry gaze was no longer that of the Eric I'd known; it belonged to someone else and it swept across the farm with something close to loathing. He marched himself back down through the long pasture, swiping the heads off dandelions, cowslips and buttercups with his knotted stick. I trailed behind, at a distance.

'It may be just as possible,' he said grimly, 'to produce a new breed of men who do not wish for liberty – as to produce a new breed of hornless cows.'

He took my air gun from me and started to bang away at the crows in the elms but he only succeeded in raising a din and scattering them across the sky.

'I may have to publish it at my own expense,' he said, then marched on, his stride lengthening, his stick swishing. Suddenly he bounded forward and hammered his big boot on to something long and squirming, anchoring it to the ground.

'You realise that's an adder,' he said.

I bent to examine its markings; I had no fear of farm snakes.

'Yes, sir. We get a lot of them in summer.'

'I thought my name was George.'

I expected him to grind the adder's head with his other boot; to my astonishment, he produced his penknife, selected the longest blade, and ripped the snake open like filleting a dead fish.

'So much for Comrade Gollancz!'

Slit.

'So much for Mr Cape and his whispering time-serving imbeciles in the Ministry of Lies. Telegraphic address: MINIFORM. "Highly ill-advised to publish at the present time." You see. "Undesirable, premature, would serve no good purpose." You see. The Russians and their dictator are "touchy". You see. "Better to choose some animal other than pigs." You see. "Let the matter lie on the table as far as we are concerned." You see.'

Slit, rip.

'Did you know that MINIFORM is located in the highest building in central London, the Senate House in Malet Street? I used to be able to see it from the roof of my block of flats in St John's Wood – even the trees in Regent's Park couldn't conceal it. For some reason no bomb ever seemed to strike MINIFORM. Now why would that be?'

I didn't know why.

'And what about Messrs Faber and Faber? What about their director, the very distinguished Mr T. S. Eliot, that rare specimen, an intelligent Tory? First I offer him tramps, then it's pigs. "We have no conviction that this is the right point of view at the present time," says Mr Eliot. "I have a regard for your work, because it is good writing of fundamental integrity," Mr Eliot nobly informs me. But. But, you see.'

Rip, slit, rip. He was brooding on this Eliot.

'A second-rate circus dog turns his somersault when the trainer cracks his whip. A first-rate circus dog does it without the whip.'

The snake was filleted. There were rain clouds to the west, over Porterstone.

'So that's where we've got to in this country, thanks to three hundred years of living together without a civil war. You see.'

I was watching the remains of the adder fitfully thrashing in his large hand. Mr Blair saw my tears.

'Thought you were a tough little fellow,' he said.

'Thought you were against cruelty to animals.'

He strode off towards the pond but I didn't follow. He came back and put a hand on my shoulder. We sat down together in the long grass and I remembered how he used to talk about the richness of summer during the winter months – the songs and smells mingling and ascending – but now it gave him no pleasure.

'We don't have censorship in England, do we?' he said abruptly. It wasn't really a question.

'Dunno.' I was massacring some wild flower, steadying myself after the adder.

'I never really told you what I've been doing at the BBC. I've been engaged in unarmed combat with the Ministry of Truth. You prepare a series of talks. First one is told to go ahead, then one is choked off on the ground that the plans are "injudicious" or "premature", then one is told to go ahead again, then told to water everything down and cut out any plain statements that may have crept in – and at the last moment the whole thing is mysteriously cancelled. Between you and me, it's all balls but if I want that printed I have to write "it's all b blank s" and I'm not even allowed the correct number of blanks to indicate the number of missing letters. Otherwise our free citizens might spend their reading hours mainly counting on their fingers and moving their lips. Did I tell you what happened to me three weeks before the war began? Two police detectives knocked on the door of my cottage. They explained quite politely that they'd come to confiscate some of my books. The Obelisk Press in Paris, you see – not allowed. They took them all, Henry Miller, the lot. Afterwards they returned some of them and the Prosecutor sent me a polite note letting me off on this one occasion.'

We sat in silence. I was glad that Joe, Tom and Constable Gill hadn't known about the Prosecutor.

'My silly fairy story's probably no good anyway,' Eric finally said. 'Pigs don't read and write, do they?'

'No, sir.'

'Cart-horses don't build windmills.'

'No, sir.'

'Old Major never had a dream, did he?'

'No, sir.'

'You're not frightened of me, are you, Alex?'

'No, sir. A bit, sir.'

His arm was right round my shoulder now as he walked me down to the pond. We sat on the bank, watching the ducks, as he slowly rolled his black shag.

'As a matter of fact,' he said, 'I have something altogether bigger and nastier in mind.'

'Than what, Eric?'

'Than animal farm. Something to make Messrs Gollancz, Cape and Eliot wet their pants.'

The black clouds were now overhead. When the first drops of rain fell he said, 'Looks like thunder, did you know that Thursday means Thunder's day?' and he shifted us under the willow.

He had fallen silent now. He was jotting some thoughts in a notebook. Our black mare Mollie had her head bent to the long summer grass a few paces off. The rain bounced lightly off her hide. Mr Blair was studying her intently, his mouth set.

I watched his pencil move across the page in rapid bursts:

'1) I saw a horse called Mollie (delete) called Boxer being whipped to his feet by an army officer and driven to his death.

'2) Pigsoc, Pigspeak, Pighate.'

Haltingly I asked him what these words meant but no direct answer was forthcoming. All he said was:

'MINIFORM equals MINITRUE – Ministry of Truth. Of Lies. As a matter of fact I used to think well of C. K. Ogden's Basic English, everything down to eight hundred and fifty words, real meaning exposed, I thought, potential abolition of jargon, I thought, but then Churchill got keen on it – he wants to teach the colonies NEWSPEAK after the war.'

I nodded, not understanding.

'I advise you to sell the farm, Alex. I won't be able to buy it thanks to Messrs Gollancz, Cape, Eliot and Faber and Faber.'

I waited.

I hadn't told Eric that Fred had been back, close to tears, too miserable to give me a ride in the Lagonda, too down-in-the-mouth to dust the dogs' and cats' hairs off the living-room chair before he slumped into it, half-shaven, with big new bags under his eyes.

'George doesn't think of me as a first-league publisher. Does he?'

I shrugged.

'No prestige. No T. S. Eliot. I could have warned him about Gollancz! Straight into the jaws of the pro-Soviet conspiracy! Censored!'

My heart sank. Eric would never be able to buy the farm.

Fred's cigarette-holder had moved close to my ear. 'Between ourselves, Alex, what's this book of George's called?'

'I dunno, sir.' Fred's large eyes looked reproachful. He didn't believe me. 'It may be *The Talking Pigs*, sir.'

'What? Are you sure?'

'No, sir.'

Fred slapped his hands with his kid gloves, the neat oiled hair flat on his flat-backed head.

'I've even heard,' he said darkly, 'that Eliot turned it down. One of our foremost men of letters. I can only think of Gide's rejection of Proust when Gide was a reader for Gallimard.'

I nodded politely. I could see that Fred was really upset. I warmed to him a bit. I knew he was a swindler but I could tell that he really thought the world of Eric.

Fred lifted his hands to heaven in exasperation:

'Of all London publishers, he knows me best! My wife drew him in charcoal! The Home Guard together! Always comrades! And I hear he wants to publish it himself, as a "pamphlet"! But where will he get the paper? How will he persuade the booksellers to stock his little "pamphlet"? How will he secure orders from Canada, Australia, New Zealand, South Africa? I can get the paper. Does he imagine that paper falls out of the sky in time of war, like the flying bomb which destroyed our offices in Essex Street! I saw it descend! From our penthouse in Primrose Hill you can see for twenty miles right across to the North Downs. Night after night we watch as these pilotless cylinders pass to the right or left of St Paul's. Night after night we make our grim calculations on the map. The sound of an explosion travels at –'

'One thousand one hundred feet per second,' I cut in.

'Exactly. Clever boy. One night between four and five in the morning we saw an explosion in direct line with Essex Street, off the Strand. Do you know the area?'

'No, sir.'

'The explosion took eighteen seconds to reach us –'

'Nineteen thousand eight hundred feet is six thousand three hundred yards is three miles one thousand and twenty yards.'

'Exactly. My wife and I took the bus to the Strand. There was a police cordon at the top of Essex Street. I smelt the familiar musty smell of disaster. Our elegant Georgian building of dark grey brick was a heap of rubble. Everything was gone. The caretaker had been killed in the basement.'

'Rotten luck,' I said.

Fred let out a long, scented sigh. 'Alex, you are my scout! Secker & Warburg needs a great book, a great book! Persuade our mutual friend to send it to me and I promise you – '

A pause.

'What?'

'I promise you a royalty on every copy out of my own pocket!'

'Would you like me to wash your car?'

But now I was sitting beside a silent, brooding Eric, butcher of adders.

I said: 'Fred was here.'

Eric barely seemed to hear me.

'Fred said his office was destroyed by a flying bomb. Is that true?'

Eric nodded. 'Demolished.'

'So he can't publish your book, can he? Though he said he could find the paper. Does it take so much paper to make a book?'

Eric smiled grimly. 'Occasionally the swindlers publish more than one copy, you see.'

'Oh – yes. Thousands, you mean!'

'Fred's a brave fellow. He doesn't lie down.'

'Maybe you could help him get started again.'

'Hm.'

'Why won't you give your book to Fred?'

There was a long silence. 'It may be a question of prestige. A novel is literature, you see. Fred's mainly political. He has a few foreign novelists, Thomas Mann, but nothing much from the contemporary English scene. If you put a picture in the wrong frame people may not notice it ... or value it so highly. But we can forget about literature, can't we? It all comes down to politics, doesn't it?'

I weighed this with all the understanding I could muster.

'So you might give your book to Fred after all?'

'Hm.' Eric gave me a slow, affectionate glance. 'Alex, there's something I have to tell you. Eileen would prefer us to adopt a small baby which would grow up with us from its infancy, you see, a child without memories of other parents.' A pause. 'But I'd like you to come and stay with us in London ... when the war's over ... when it's safe, you see.'

I nodded. 'When will that be?'

'They're sending me abroad as a war correspondent. I'll write you a postcard from the Rhine.'

Then he looked at his watch. He didn't stay for tea but he left behind him a hoard of jam, Gentlemen's Relish, Cadbury's chocolate and Lyons cake, plus another shirt and a pair of new black shoes. And a one-pound note.

When the postcard arrived it was from Paris, not the Rhine. It said he'd met a writer called Hemingway, who'd also been in Spain, and who was now a war correspondent like himself. Hemingway had produced a bottle of whisky from under his bed. Eric hoped I was well. He didn't say anything about the farm or about his book. The card was signed 'E. A. Blair'. I wanted to write back to him but there was no address.

CHAPTER X

By the time *Animal Farm* appeared Mr Cripps – Colonel Cripps – had taken over Manor Farm, having licked Adolf single-handed in some hush-hush airborne intelligence unit (or so he confided to me). My mum had finally been forced to sell by auction, scotching Pilkington and Frederick's rival schemes to filch our property on the cheap, but she turned paler than pale when it turned out that Ellen's dad had got it. I thought she was going to be sick on the spot.

But the colonel was dead keen to 'make a go' of it and kindly found us better lodgings in the village, informing me rather grandly that I'd always be welcome to visit the farm because even the most 'progressive' mixed-farming methods could benefit from 'a spot of native folklore'.

He overlooked the native witchcraft.

My mum forbade me to go near the farm but of course I couldn't help myself. I noticed that Cripps's courtesies stopped short of ever inviting me into the house and I reckoned this must be because of Ellen. I don't know what she had told her dad about certain events, but whenever she visited the farm, dressed in stylish London clothes, she never gave me a glance. I might have been a tree-stump. Sometimes she bought smart young gents with her, the 'hoa hoa I say good lawd' sort, and one of them once asked me whether I was the son of a hired hand 'or whatever'. But even as I was being honoured by his attention the Lady Ellen swept into the house carrying Harrods bags loaded with new lampshades, curtains and cushions.

One Saturday Cripps himself cornered me in the tractor shed and advised me to make myself scarce when Ellen was around.

I drew my sleeve across my nose.

I could tell he was embarrassed. Cripps was loudly 'progressive' all round and confided to me that he would have stood as a Labour candidate for Parliament but for some 'diehard prejudices' among farm labourers against the land-owning classes. His first step was to hire two farmhands and splash out on a new tractor, threshing machine and generator. His giant chain-saw was the first I'd ever seen and took two men to handle it. In fact farming was only a sideline for Cripps: he and his wife spent much of their time up in London 'or whatever'.

One day he handed me a small parcel addressed to myself, care of the farm.

'Feels like a book,' I said.

'If it feels like a book and looks like a book it may be a book, Alex.'

For some reason I wanted to be alone when I unwrapped it because I never received parcels and I felt it was something special and private. But Cripps was standing over my shoulder as I cut the string with my penknife.

'Ah yes,' Cripps said, lighting his Attlee pipe as the title and author came into view. 'A good writer, I'm told, though something of a maverick.'

I didn't know the word and I'd never heard of the author, though his name found an echo in some corner of my mind.

'Looks brand new,' I murmured.

Cripps smiled indulgently. 'So who could have sent it to you?'

'Dunno, sir.'

'Why not look inside? There may be a message.'

Sure enough, there was a handwritten line scribbled across the title page – a line I shall never forget: 'To Alex from E. A. Blair – with apologies and best wishes.'

'Who's E. A. Blair?' Cripps asked.

'He's my friend, sir.'

Cripps tactfully inquired no further. 'Hope you enjoy it,' he said, moving off in his brilliant brown army boots. 'Though I must say it's an odd title.'

I took the book home in its brown-paper wrapping, and shut myself in my room after supper when my mum settled down to her ironing and usual radio rubbish. I couldn't believe it! I was amazed to find so many details exactly corresponding to Manor Farm, the farmhouse furniture, the barn, the small paddock beyond the orchard, the knoll in the long pasture, the ruined windmill, the ploughland, hayfield, pool and spinney. But the story itself was completely made-up and utterly fantastic from beginning to end.

I read it right through without a pause. It was one of the best stories I'd ever read – ever written, I reckon.

I didn't dare show it to my mum. Because of the names. Almost all of the names, people and animals, were real. And the book was full of horrible lies about my dad.

– Jones too drunk to shut the pop-holes

– Jones drowning his old dogs in the pond by tying a brick round their necks

– Jones spending whole days lounging in the Windsor chair in the kitchen, drinking

– Jones slumped in the taproom of the Red Lion at 'Willingdon' (Porterstone), complaining to anyone who would listen

– Jones dying in a home for 'inebriates' (I had to look this word up in my dad's Collins Dictionary)

Angry though I was, bafflement was my main emotion. I had little doubt that Eric was somehow behind this fairy story, and must have told his tale in all innocence to one of his clever London friends, Mr George Orwell. That would explain Eric's scribbled message to me: 'with apologies'.

During my next visit to the farm I found Cripps tinkering lovingly with his new red tractor. He beckoned me over.

'Well, did you read it?'

'Yes, sir.'

'So did I. Bought a copy. Not bad, eh? In fact, a highly progressive book. It's an allegory, of course, very much in the tradition of Swift.'

'What's that, sir?'

'An allegory? You say one thing and mean another.'

'What did he mean, then?'

'History of the Soviet Union. I'm surprised they let him publish it. Well, the war's over now. Even so, we don't want to offend our Russian friends, do we?'

'No, sir.'

'I looked him up in the library, Alex.'

'Who, sir?'

'George Orwell. Real name Eric Blair. Pseudonyms are quite common in the literary game. So it seems your copy is signed by the author himself. Could become valuable. Hang on to it.' Cripps chortled. 'I dare say some of our neighbours won't be too pleased. I noticed Orwell changed Porterstone to Willingdon but he didn't bother to change much else.'

'Oh yes he did, sir!' I burst out.

Cripps placed a kindly hand on my head. 'About your father, you mean? Hm.'

'It's a pack of lies, sir!'

'I'm sure it is. Don't let it worry you, Alex. You know what these writers are like.'

I didn't – and I didn't like the bag of plums in Cripps's mouth, either. Of course he despised us. This gent had been having his good war when my parents suffered their troubles, and it was ten to one that he believed the rotten things Eric had written about my dad – what with Ellen and everything, though of course Eric hadn't written anything about that. The Jones family were for pity and charity, that was it. Eric had been happy enough to sit on my dad's Windsor chair, drinking his vile black brew of tea out of my mum's Crown Derby cups (or saucers), while pretending to be my friend. That 'with apologies' was a bit rich. I wanted to write back to Eric and tell him what I thought of him, but each time I started a letter I tore it up and I think I felt more flattered than anything that I had known a famous author and he'd written about our farm. I carried the book with me wherever I went.

One hot summer day I was fishing for carp beneath the willow while browsing through the scene in which Knacker Simmonds carries Boxer away. Eric could almost have been sitting there next to me, rolling his shag. I often thought about him. Anyway, I stretched out, fell asleep, and pitched into a dream I shall never forget.

I dreamed I was asleep under the willow tree. Eric's book had slipped from my hand. In my dream I woke up in the late afternoon, with the air cooling and the shadows beginning to lengthen. I noticed Boxer and Clover grazing in the meadow, not far away. I reached out for Eric's book but it was gone. I reckoned Cripps must have picked it up, so I called at the farmhouse.

He shrugged. 'You should be more careful of your possessions, Alex.' Meaning, of course, that my dad should have been more careful with the farm. I went off in a black mood because I reckoned Cripps had stolen my copy, what with it having the message and signature in it.

Two days later I found the book lying in the yard, tatty and jawed and pawed and trottered. But it wasn't my copy, it didn't have the message in it. I tossed it to the pigs. I saw Snowball sniffing it shiftily. He was definitely pretending not to be interested. Napoleon's slit eyes gleamed for a moment. Squealer suddenly scampered in his sty. Later I came across other mucky copies in the big barn, in the kennels and sties and coops. Call me a liar, but Manor Farm was littered with copies of *Animal Farm*.

I didn't tell Cripps. I saw no reason to. I was watching him carefully but generally keeping out of his way. I noticed his temper was fraying. He was shouting at his farmhands. He had a haggard and sleepless look. Any moment and he would bite right through his Attlee pipe. One of the new hired hands, Jack, told me that Cripps was beginning to 'talk daft about Bolshie pigs and dangerous dogs.'

Cripps found me in the yard later the same day.

'Alex!'

'Sir?'

'Come here!'

'Sir?'

'So what's going on?'

'On, sir?'

He was walking in small circles. 'You swear you don't know a thing, is that it?'

'About what, sir?'

'The behaviour of the animals. Come, boy, don't pretend you haven't seen copies of that damned book lying all over the place.'

'No, sir. But I told you, sir, I lost the copy Mr Blair sent me, I left it under the willow.'

'Alex, they're reading it,' Cripps said darkly.

'Reading it, sir! Animals can't read!'

'I suspect they regard Orwell as some kind of prophet or soothsayer,' he muttered. 'Stupid buggers. It isn't a prophecy, it's a warning. And it isn't about f— animals either.'

From Cripps's lips such a word was shocking and when he went back into the house you could hear him shouting at his wife, which wasn't normally his style at all. Then he came out again, started shooting at rooks and crows, then drove off to the doctor to get himself an anti-rabies injection.

Jack told me he and the other hand were regularly getting bitten – both of them had been given injections by the doctor. Animals I'd known all their lives were turning Bolshie. Napoleon, Snowball and Squealer were now far more vicious than during those long months when they were growing hungrier and squealing for mash in dead of winter.

Although Cripps now padlocked his splendid new tractor and threshing machine during the night, they were regularly got at. I remembered Eric explaining 'sabotage'. In the morning nothing was where Cripps or Jack had left it the night before.

Ellen arrived at the weekend with one of her Brilliantined whatevers in tow. I heard the car approaching from the five-barred gate and hid myself in the shadows behind the harness room. When she got out of her Triumph sports car with wing mirrors and five front lamps, gleaming like a goddess and showing a long stretch of silk stocking, she heard Boxer and Clover drumming with their great hairy hoofs on the stable door. I saw her hesitate, then she began to cross the yard on her high heels towards the stables. She always fancied herself with the horses.

I flicked my fingers – a very small movement. Jessie and Bluebell came streaking out of the barn. Ellen screamed. Jessie went for her silk stockings while Bluebell reared up, biting the hand that Ellen had raised to protect her face. The shock of it knocked her to the ground. Cripps came hurtling out of the house, gun in hand, but he couldn't shoot because the dogs were on top of Ellen. The Brilliantined whatever from London was standing by the wing mirrors and five front lamps, mouth open.

Cripps rushed his daughter to the doctor while I fed Jessie and Bluebell from a packet of biscuits, behind the harness room. Then I made myself scarce, avoiding the road and cutting across the fields.

A few days later I was helping Jack load up Boxer and Clover with firewood when Colonel Cripps grabbed me by the collar.

'We're going for a walk,' he said. He more or less frog-marched me down to the long pasture, constantly glancing up at the trees with bloodshot eyes, as if to make sure that the crows and ravens weren't listening.

'Listen, young Jones. I suspect you know more about all this than you're letting on.'

'No, sir. What, sir? How's Ellen, sir?'

'Ah! How come you know about that?'

'Jack told me she got bit, sir.'

'Hm. She was lucky to get out alive. But that's nothing to what happened last night.'

'What, sir?'

Cripps lit his pipe. 'You won't believe this – or perhaps you will.' He gave me a nasty look. 'I'd secured the hen-houses and taken myself to bed when I heard something ... something.'

'What, sir?'

'Stop saying "What, sir?"! I heard an extraordinary stirring and fluttering all through the farm buildings. Everywhere! So after a while I got up and soft-footed it down to the barn. I looked through the door and what did I find? Old Major, our placid twelve-year-old boar, was ensconced on a bed of straw, surrounded by the other pigs, the dogs Bluebell, Jessie and Pincher, the cart-horses – oh yes, Boxer and Clover were there – the donkeys and goats – the lot! Old Major started snorting and grunting and then he began to ... began to ...'

'To what, sir?'

'To sing, damn it! And all the other animals in the wildest excitement began to sing with him!'

'But animals can't *sing*, sir!'

He looked down at me with the nastiest expression. '*Your* good friend Mr Orwell tells us that they can sing. He even writes the lyrics for them, very obliging.'

I shrugged. 'So what did you do, sir?'

His smile was now rather bleak. 'Nothing, Alex. I'm a Labour man, you see.'

'Yes, sir.'

'If we have social democracy for men, perhaps we should extend it to animals. I'm not a tyrannical farmer like your ...

hm. We must use our reason. Be progressive. Fabians like myself believe in discussion – debate, eh? Health, education, welfare, that's the key and I know what I'm talking about. I've seen a bit of the world, you know. Horizons round here are pretty narrow, I'd say. If we finally have to go to the new Arbitration Board, so be it.'

Clearly Cripps was off his rocker but I nodded respectfully and he cheered up and took himself off to drink his tea out of my parents' Crown Derby.

I visited the farm two days later. From the moment I vaulted the five-barred gate I could tell that things were getting worse. There was no sign of Jack or the other hand. The windows of the farmhouse were boarded up. Dogs I knew well followed me growling and snarling, as if I were a stranger. Boxer and Clover reared up when my hand reached for their noses.

'So what's got into you?' I asked them.

The great beasts were sweating and trembling in their stalls. Clover sort of nudged Boxer and they quieted down enough to accept a couple of apples from my hand. Then I went back to the yard and told the dogs to pack it in and they slunk away. Jessie and Bluebell took biscuits from my hand. I walked across to the sties. Old Major was asleep but Napoleon and Snowball were clearly keen to bite my head clean off. I yelled at them – they knew that yell but they didn't cower. I tossed them some swill from a bucket but they wouldn't touch it. That had never happened before – these were pigs, after all.

I knocked on the farmhouse door. You could hear the heavy bolt and key being turned. Cripps opened the door a crack. I could see he'd installed an iron chain. He had a gun in his hand.

'Ah,' he said, 'it's you. They've established a soviet in the sties.'

'A what, sir?'

'It's definitely a soviet.' After a moment Cripps emerged cautiously into the yard, glancing around like a haunted man. He was clearly at the end of his rope. He walked like a cripple from his bites and rabies injections. I followed him down to the long pasture where we sat down on a log and he lit his pipe – one of Eric's favourite spots for rolling his black shag.

'Alex,' he sighed, 'there isn't a single trader in Porterstone any longer willing to call here. Even that bloody knacker, Simmonds, is refusing. Look.' He rolled up his trousers to the knee; I saw that his lower leg was covered with vicious bites, scratches, brown iodine and sticking plasters.

'Phew,' I said.

'I'm a rationalist myself,' Cripps said, 'but I believe these stupid creatures are under some kind of voodoo or curse. It's that book. Follow me?'

'Well . . .'

'What we need is an exorcism. I don't go to church much myself but, frankly, I see no alternative. And I want you to hand.'

'Why, sir?'

'Because you know these bloody animals better than anyone. I've got eyes in my head, you know.'

'But I have to go to school, sir.'

Cripps dug in his pocket and handed me a pound note.

The following day the Reverend Goodfellow turned up in his full fancy dress, vestments, chalice, the lot, with Cripps in attendance, a gun under one arm and me under the other. The vicar then murmured to him about the gun.

'Trust in God but keep your powder dry, Vicar,' Cripps barked in his most soldierly manner.

Father Goodfellow halted at the five-barred gate beyond which were massed almost all of the farm's larger animals, teeth bared, throats growling, tails lashing.

'You see, Father, they're possessed! Possessed!' exclaimed Cripps.

'Indeed, indeed,' the vicar sighed.

'Ask this boy here,' Cripps said, pointing to me but not dignifying me with a name, 'he knows these animals well. Have you ever seen them in such a state, boy?'

'No, sir.'

'Indeed,' the vicar sighed again, tilting his two chins down to his breast, obviously terrified by the snarling, lowing, snorting and braying beyond the gate. Then he began speaking from memory in his rather high, posh voice – it sounded to me as if he was sucking a gallon of fizzy lemonade through a dozen drinking straws.

'Again, the devil taketh him up into an exceeding high mountain, and sheweth him all the kingdoms of the world, and the glory of them; And saith unto him, All these things will I give thee, if thou wilt fall down and worship me. Then saith Jesus unto him, Get thee hence, Satan . . .'

(I can't pretend I got all the spelling and punctuation as I listened to the Reverend Goodfellow – and I can't pretend I listened at all. I never listened in church, the few times I went, though the vicar had wanted me to be a choirboy in the days when the Joneses were still respectable.)

Our old cow Gertie lowed; she'd calved recently – her seventh – and her udder was practically touching the ground. I noticed the big boars Napoleon and Snowball shifting their fifteen-stone hulks restlessly on their trotters, but it was the dogs who seemed to have the devils in them. Quite suddenly the Reverend Goodfellow began tossing water from his chalice over the fence at the dogs while coming out with a language I didn't know but sounding a bit like this:

'*Inimice fidei, hostis generis humani, mortis adductor, vitae raptor, causa discordiae* ... '

It was some kind of set-piece for baptising dogs, I guessed, but it didn't go down any better than the waters of Jordan slopping over their arched backs and rearing heads. They certainly didn't look baptised. I noticed that Colonel Cripps was sulking a bit, as if the vicar had forgotten he was C of E or something. I frankly didn't think Father Goodfellow was doing himself a favour with the foreign stuff, and crossing himself all the time, and lifting his chalice to the sky, which seemed foreign as well, and he must have had the same thought because he quickly flipped open his Bible and resumed his drinking-straw voice:

'And when he was come to the other side into the country of the Gerg-ge-senes, there met him two possessed with devils, coming out of their tombs, exceeding fierce, so that no man might pass by that way.'

Even I got the point of that – and the colonel was looking less like a haystack about to catch fire. 'That's more like it,' he growled. 'Give it to 'em, Vicar.'

'And behold, they cried out, saying, What have we to do with thee, Jesus, thou Son of God? Art thou come hither to torment us before the time?'

The Reverend Goodfellow paused rather smugly (I thought); all the animals had fallen silent because they were obviously enjoying the story – though Gertie's milk-moaning was unstoppable.

'And there was a good way off from them a herd of many

swine feeding,' declared the vicar with what you might have taken for a smirk. Our pigs were certainly dead interested to find themselves in the Bible. You could have heard a pin drop. The ears of the big boars were twitching like mad.

'So the devils besought him, saying, If thou cast us out, suffer us to go away into the herd of swine.' The vicar paused dramatically. 'And he said unto them, Go.'

'Wait a minute,' Cripps muttered. 'The devils are in my swine already. No need to pack more in.'

But Father Goodfellow was unstoppable:

'And when they were come out, they went into the herd of swine: and behold the whole herd of swine ran violently down a steep place into the sea and perished in the waters.'

'Are you mad, Vicar!' Cripps bellowed, his jowls gorged with blood; simultaneously a devilish snorting, snarling, growling and braying arose beyond the fence. 'Let me have a go, you nit! Fire is what these devils fear – hellfire!' The colonel was now busy dousing a brand new copy of *Animal Farm* in paraffin. After breaking half a dozen matches he managed to set the book alight, and tossed it over the fence, aiming for the pigs. The vicar seemed rather shocked but, strangely enough, the animals fell into a deep silence. The sheep and goats drew back a few paces from the burning book, while the fowl fluttered away – but the dogs stood their ground, in silence, tongues lolling.

'That's fixed the buggers. Open the gate, Alex,' Cripps commanded me, cocking his gun. He and the vicar both stepped aside to allow me this privilege.

I hesitated a second or two, knees knocking and all that. As bad luck would have it, at the moment I opened the gate another pack of dogs led by Bluebell and Jessie tore out of the loft over the harness room, raced across the yard towards us with dripping jaws, then sank their teeth into Cripps and the vicar, chasing them down the road and out of sight like hounds in pursuit of badgers. I heard several sharp reports from Cripps's gun. Presently the dogs returned at a more leisurely pace, carrying shreds of clothing between their teeth and dragging three of their wounded comrades. (It is of course impossible for a dog to do this, but I saw it with my own eyes.)

I noticed that Jessie and Bluebell were not among the returning dogs and feared that they must be dead. But, cycling down the road perhaps four hundred yards, I found the two bitches pinning Cripps and the vicar in a ditch by the throat. I merely spoke their names and they drew back, growling.

'Go!' I commanded. They hesitated, then obediently trotted up the road towards the farm.

'Oh thank you, thank you, dear boy,' moaned the Reverend Goodfellow, searching the grass verge for his Bible, his chalice and his purple stole. But Cripps was far from thankful. He grabbed me by the ear.

'You've got some explaining to do, young sir, and you'd f— well better start now.'

He wanted to know why I never got bitten. He wanted to know why I had left a copy of *Animal Farm* lying beneath the willow – he called this '*your* story'. In short Cripps accused me of deliberately stirring rebellion among the animals by hurling copies of Mr Orwell's book at them.

'They didn't f— well bicycle into the f— village and f— buy it for themselves,' he yelled. 'You want this f— farm back, don't you, young Jones, ha? Now you've had my money, Master Jones, you and your mother – '

He might have throttled me on the spot had not the vicar

intervened, rebuking him for his foul language to 'an innocent child who saved our lives.'

When I returned to the farm several nights later, approaching across the fields under cover of darkness, it had been abandoned. Cripps had fled. I found the farmhouse door wide open and the rooms vandalised; furniture which had once belonged to my parents was smashed, including my dad's favourite Pembroke table, with fold-down wings. There was pig shit all over the Wilton carpet in the living-room. The beer barrel in the scullery had been stove in by one of Boxer's giant, hairy hoofs. I cleaned up the mess as best I could then settled down for the night behind locked doors and windows.

Back in my own bed after so many weeks' exile, it wasn't easy to sleep. I remembered what my dad had always said: 'You work hard and you sell hard – no one takes what is yours.'

I thought about my dad and Ellen. I thought about Mr Blair, who'd become Eric and wanted to be George. I still wasn't having George. Despite all the lies in his book, if Eric now came striding up the road, with his big boots and haggard face and loaded rucksack, I'd still call him Eric. Maybe he would come back. I fell asleep watching Eric sitting on a log in the long pasture, rolling his black shag.

I must have slept late. The house was very quiet. I didn't hear a sound from the yard outside. I went to the window and wiped the dew from the pane. And then I saw them, waiting for me in total silence: every creature on the farm had gathered in the yard and was gazing intently up at my bedroom window.

When I stepped out of the front door it was old Boxer who first approached me, steam gushing from his nostrils in the cool morning air, shrouding the thick white line down his nose. He stopped a few paces from me and I saw that he'd lost one of his shoes. Then his mate Clover came forward slowly and stood beside him.

'Good morning, comrade,' Boxer said.

'Good morning, comrade,' I said. 'Now lift your hoof and let's see what's happened to your shoe.'

Boxer was about to obey but the fifteen-stone boar, Snowball, darted forward a few paces with that surprising speed which even the heaviest of pigs can display.

'Don't lift your foot, Comrade Boxer,' Snowball commanded. 'We no longer take orders from humans.'

There was an intense silence in the yard.

I flicked my fingers at Jessie and Bluebell. Their backs arched with the strain of denying my authority, but they didn't move. I produced a couple of biscuits from my pocket but they held their ground, hungry though they were.

The cows' udders hung swollen and unmilked; their legs were trembling with discomfort, but when I moved towards them they backed away, snorting.

Now the great Berkshire boar Napoleon stepped forward and I woke up with a start beneath the willow tree, with the summer air cooling and the shadows lengthening, my head still crammed with the dream. Eric's book was lying in the grass beside me. A few yards away Boxer and Clover were grazing placidly. I noticed that Boxer's shoes were all in good order. I heard distant voices from the direction of the farmhouse, Ellen's laughter, and then Cripps's giant chainsaw started up in the spinney.

I cycled home. It was the last time I set foot on Manor Farm until it became mine again many years later.

CHAPTER XI

One day, about two years later, a large brown envelope arrived. It was addressed to me care of Porterstone Post Office and it was postmarked 'Jura', which sounded foreign, though our King's head was on the stamps. Inside the envelope I found some typed pages and a letter.

Dear Alex,

I had an odd idea recently. I'm living up here on an island in northern Scotland. The house looks out on to the sea. It's not always easy to keep warm but I think you would take to it like a duck to water. There's no shortage of fishing. When one gets decent weather one can go out in the boat. On the west side of the island you find uninhabited bays, white sand and seals swimming about. But you have to be alert for the tides and one or two whirlpools. I spend quite a lot of time mending and caulking the boat, which has an outboard motor. Recently we got into difficulty in a heavy swell and had to swim for it (with my small boy under my arm). Luckily there was an island. I went off to look for some puffins' eggs but they're curious birds and live in burrows. I expect you would have enjoyed this adventure, including the near-disaster, although it occurs to me that you may never have learned to swim. You must be a big fellow by now and not so easy to save as my small son.

Here's the odd idea I had. I imagined you reading *Animal Farm* beneath that willow tree by your old pond. Do you still visit the farm? (I wonder whether you did read the book, or ever received it.) I imagined you falling asleep in the long grass and the book slipping from your hand. Anyway, I have started a story based on this idea, which I am sending you. Don't bother with it if you have better things to do. The question in my mind is whether we can avoid outright slavery and the division of the world into two or three super-states.

I hope you are now at the grammar school. I'm told that all grammar school places have been free and based on a competitive entrance examination since the 1944 Education Act. However, I rarely believe what I'm told. I remember discussing this with you but I don't clearly recall what you said. They promised they would put an end to the old elementary schools, but I hear reports that in some areas this has gone no further than a new lick of paint and a new sign-board. If you are still at the elementary school, which I believe they now call a secondary modern, what hope have you of taking the School Certificate? This new-fangled stuff about 'Ourselves and Our Districts', 'Ourselves and Our World', is no better than the old-fashioned courses in woodwork and metalwork, which at least had some practical usefulness.

I hope you are well.

With best wishes,

Yours,

E. A. Blair.

There was no address on Eric's letter. I read his typed story. It was called 'The Last Man' but this had been struck out and replaced, in Eric's hand, by 'The Willow Tree'.

It was another fairy story about our farm and our animals but this time Eric had put me right in the middle of it, though he didn't call me Alex. I was called Winston Jones, which became Winston Smith with a stroke of the pen, Jones and Smith no doubt being 'figures of speech' (as Fred had so candidly put it). All the same, I may have been a bit flattered to be written about, though Eric's 'the boy' struck me as more like his design for a windmill than a real one. There was probably a big hidden message but it was beyond me. I was tempted to show it to my English master, Boothroyd, a heaving Orwell fan, but didn't.

Another two years had passed when the new book arrived. It was waiting for me at the post office. Even before I opened the parcel I felt sure it was from Eric because no one else sent me parcels. I thought it might be the rest of 'The Willow Tree' but the title was different and there was nothing about our farm. This time there was no inscription from E. A. Blair, just a printed slip from the publishers, Secker & Warburg, 'With the compliments of the Author', and some words added by the swindler:

> Dear Alex, George asked me to send this to you with his best wishes. Unfortunately he's not very well at the moment and cannot personally sign as many copies as he would like to. Our mutual friend is now very famous, as you may know, and fame is a mixed blessing. Do write to him through this address – it will cheer him up. All the best, Fredric Warburg.

It took me quite some time to get through Eric's new book, though I never quite did. You couldn't help admiring his gift for invention, the Ministry of Love without any windows, and the new language which meant the opposite of what it said, but for my money it wasn't a patch on *Animal Farm*. His animal characters were altogether more lively and 'human' than his human beings. (I may have felt a bit disappointed that he'd abandoned 'The Willow Tree', which had ended in mid-sentence just when 'the boy' was about to make a big decision.) And there was a lot of heavy, dull stuff in the new book. Shoved right into the middle was a lump of concrete called 'The Theory and Practice of Oligarchical Collectivism' by Emmanuel Goldstein (obviously another you know what). The more I tried to get through it the more often I fiddled with my acne, squeezing puss and dabbing the hated spots with Ma Pyke's Somerset Remedy. I still had a few copies of *Autocar*, *Motor* and *Autosport*, and generally found these mags a good distraction from 'The Theory and Practice of Oligarchical Collectivism'. My eye did fasten on one passage when Winston Smith sits in bed after shagging Julia, reading E. Goldstein to her page after page – and then finally notices she's fast asleep, 'naked from the waist upwards'. You couldn't blame her.

There had been no dirty stuff in *Animal Farm* and I didn't expect any from Eric. I remembered him talking about having a girl on the hard, frosted ground in some park, but that had seemed sort of distant and manly, not sloppy and undignified, like Winston following Julia while carrying a bunch of bluebells and studying the curve of her hips. Then it's bodies melting, a woman as yielding as water, mouths clinging together. 'He pressed her down upon the grass, among the fallen bluebells.'

And when he presses her down, it's Manor Farm all over again. Rutting beside a stream with big fish. 'You can watch them lying in the pools under the willow trees, waving their tails,' he says or she says. Eric certainly knew how to make several meals out of a minnow. And I noticed the sneer about cheap porn, *Spanking Stories* and *One Night in a Girls' School*, 'bought furtively by proletarian youths'.

That was me. Two years ago Eric had 'hoped' I was at the grammar school. Why should I be? He had also hoped that all grammar school places were now free, but 'I rarely believe what I'm told'. What did he believe? It was definitely time for this 'proletarian youth' to pick the lice out of his hair and rite a leter.

Dear Eric,

Many thanks for 1984. It's brileant. I liked the bit about the cloks stricking thirtheen. I fownd all the gloom and doom a bit over the top. What hapened to the story you seant me, 'The Willow Tree'. I didn't understand all the politiks but I liked the way our donky Benjamin kept saying, 'Wich paje are we on.' I escpect Benjamin is ded by now, and Boxer and Clover to. I am very sorry that you are ill. Congratlatns on saving your smal son from drowing. My English marster at the grammer school Boothroyd says you're very famus now. He wouldn't beleeve I'd known you once until I showd him my sighned copy of Animal Farm. He oferd me five kwid for it. Sorry about the speling. I'm still best at maths.

Yours sinserly,

Alex Jones.

One day I'd slouched out of Porterstone Grammar School

for the lunch break (Sixth Form privilege, but no pubs, no girls, etc.) when I saw a flash Jaguar parked outside. Fred climbed out, unwrapping his right hand. I took it cordially.

'How do you do, sir? Nice to see you after so long.'

Fred beamed at my courtesy, despite my stained black blazer and flannels, my horribly scuffed shoes, the toe-caps worn grey by playing football for England. Matthews to Mortensen to Carter to Lawton! Lawton with his head! It's a goal! England one, Scotland nil!

'Got rid of the Lagonda, did you, sir? Pity you didn't offer it to me.'

He chortled and embraced me awkwardly, smelling of oriental hair oil and sandalwood soap.

'Alex,' he said. 'Dear Alex. So long – but no longer the small boy of yesteryear. A young man.'

I wondered what he'd expected: hibernation?

'So Eric let you publish *Animal Farm* after all?' I winked nastily.

'Sorry?'

'Have you forgotten your much appreciated mendicant visitations to the farm?'

Fred looked distinctly uneasy.

'Ah. Well, of course it was a hard, a very hard decision for us to make. My wife said she'd leave me if I published it. The Russians had shouldered most of the fighting since 1941. It took courage to go ahead. I wouldn't have done it for any author but George. A dozen American publishers turned it down ...'

'Come to reward your "scout", have you?'

Fred reached for his cigarette case. Now came a story about a pub he'd frequented off the Strand during the war, half-decent food. 'George' rushes in looking like a refugee, out of breath, whips a thin typescript in a flimsy brown paper wrapper from his briefcase, explains that he has only a minute to spare – then vanishes.

'Well, thank you for telling me,' I said.

Fred's big eyes brimmed. 'Alex, our mutual friend George doesn't have long.'

'Why?'

'He wants to see you, Alex. Advanced TB. He got your letter. I've spoken to your headmaster, leave is granted.'

'Why should Eric want to see me?'

There were kids watching us; the smart gent with the leaping chrome Jag on his bonnet – and the nose – was attracting rustic attention on a large scale, but I was in no hurry, didn't mind. Fred thought he could just conjure me away on four cylinders, but I needed six. I asked him again: why should Eric want to see *me*?

'Guilt and grief, Alex. George doesn't wear success lightly, you know. He's still the knight of the woeful countenance.'

'I don't expect his wife would want me around.'

'Eileen? She died four years ago.'

'Oh.'

'He married again last week – from his hospital bed.'

'He must be happy, then. Give him my congratulations.'

'A dying man is less than happy,' Fred said with dignity. 'Despite one million copies of *Animal Farm* sold in Penguin paperback and rising – forty thousand hardcover copies of *Nineteen Eighty-Four* sold in this country alone – plus a hundred and seventy thousand in the USA – plus a hundred and ninety thousand issued by the Book of the Month Club. Alex, please climb in, please do, we're late already.'

'That sounds like a lot of pluses, Fred. So who needs socialism?'

Fred looked pained. His voice fell to a hoarse whisper. 'I hope you will not make such remarks to George.'

'You haven't done too badly, Fred.'

'Don't believe that. George is now on seventeen and a half per cent of six shillings. Paper and printing cost me over a shilling, the booksellers take two shillings ...'

'You forgot my royalty.'

Fred anxiously examined his gold watch. 'Alex, there is no time to lose. I've made a special appointment at the hospital.'

'How will I get back, then?'

'There's a seven-fifteen train. I'll pay the fare.' Fred looked at my stains, my frayed cuffs and scuffed shoes, hesitated, then pushed me into the car.

'I haven't had my dinner,' I said.

'We'll pick up something on the way.'

Fred drove with one hand on the wheel. The other, also gloved, whirled and danced expressively. I was hungry.

Fred was telling me, with awe, how 'George' had refused, adamantly and stoically refused, to bow to the Book of the Month Club and remove Emmanuel Goldstein's drivel.

'I admit I never got through that bit,' I mumbled.

'Who did?' Fred said, his face creasing into a hundred smiles. 'Unreadable! But genius knows its way. With forty thousand bucks at stake, George said no. I trembled. But the Club climbed down. Do you know what George said?'

'What?'

'George gave me his wintry smile. "That shows," he said, "that virtue is its own reward or honesty is the best policy, I forget which." '

'"Which page are we on, comrades?"'

One of Fred's big-fish eyes removed itself from his rear mirror and settled on me.

'What do you mean?'

'Didn't he show you "The Willow Tree"?'

'Ah. "The Last Man." I remember. You're right, Alex. The donkey Benjamin becomes, *faute de mieux*, the last hope. "A nod's as good as a wink," he brays –'

'Says.'

'Says. But I was only allowed a glimpse of the typescript, one quick reading, before he sent it to you for your comments.'

'He didn't ask for my comments.'

'He was very hurt you never responded. George never asks for anything.'

'He didn't even put his address.'

'Reply care of the publisher, it's standard practice. I hope you've kept "The Last Man", Alex.'

'Worth a fortune, is it?'

'George was finding his way to *Nineteen Eighty-Four*. One foot on your farm, the other on Airstrip One. A step into the abyss. The Party emerges. There is no Party in *Animal Farm* – perhaps that never struck you.'

'I'm thick.'

'George was travelling from the fallibility of human nature, down into the Burnhamite managerial revolution, and finally to total de-humanisation – the systematisation of terror. Understand?'

'Yeah. "He pressed her down upon the grass, among the fallen bluebells."'

Fred looked really upset by that. You'd have thought we'd run into another herd of cows.

'George put you into that story as a symbol of resistance, the "last man", Winston' he said.

'Jones deleted Smith, you mean?'

'In the figure of Winston, George is wrestling with the fine line between the bearable and the unbearable. That's why our hearts sink – literally! – when Winston is shown the caged rats in Room 101 and betrays the woman he loves. "Do it to Julia," he says. "Don't do it to me." That's a line of genius.'

'I reckoned Eric had more guts than that.'

'He told me he'd never known anyone braver than you, Alex.'

'Nah. I haven't had my dinner, by the way.'

Fred gave me a worried, calculating look, as if working out whether I was about to be sick all over his leather upholstery from sheer starvation. Again he studied his watch.

'We're late,' he said. 'Perhaps we can find a sandwich at a pub ...'

But we never found a pub, let alone a sandwich, though we were passing the big mock-Tudor sort that Eric so hated as we approached London. Loads of them. If Fred wasn't hungry, nobody was.

'I believe that book could have been written only by a terminally sick man,' he was saying. 'One expects Swift's savagery from George, but not the depths of Dostoevsky. Goodbye socialism, goodbye hope. Worth a cool million votes to the Conservative Party, that book. But now, of course, George keeps issuing countervailing statements from his hospital bed. "It *could* happen," he says. "Don't let it happen," he says. "It depends on *you*." Would you let it happen, Alex?'

'What, Big Brother? We saw off Adolf, didn't we?'

'Fighting Germans is easy.'

'In the Home Guard, you mean?'

'Tell me this: have you ever found yourself in a minority of one? That's the test. Have you ever stood up at school and advocated an unpopular opinion? Called for the abolition of hanging? Denounced anti-semitism? If so, you're George's "last man".'

So! Personal testimony of the 'last man', otherwise known in the King's Head as the last lout, A. Jones. Out of school for two–three years now, scratches a living as a despised piece-time day-labourer for Pilkington, Frederick and Cripps, with a spell in the Feltenham Borstal after tossing a bucket of pig-swill over the Lady Ellen and her wing mirrors (Cripps was the presiding magistrate). A string of minor convictions, usually on-probation or bound-over. Definitely a 'proletarian youth'.

So I'm rolling a fag under the Pilkington hedge when the gleaming Jag glides up. Guess who. I don't budge. I'm making steady progress with my fifth bottle of Worthington. Fred climbs out and stares at the filthy yokel with horror. I belch at both ends. His Jag's nothing to get excited about, just the 1940 S.S. model with hypoid back axles, 1.8 litres, 4 cylinders. The $3\frac{1}{2}$-litre, 6-cylinder model, with beam axles and 4-speed synchromesh gearbox, is something else, but it isn't Fred's. He's still the poor end of the Whorebergs, unwrapping his calf-skin hand and flushing a smile through his big end. I notice he's put on weight, disgusting.

'They told me where to look for you, Alex.' He's almost stammering, which isn't the Fred we know and love.

'Did *they*, mate? What's it to be then, a lit-er-ar-er-y discussion? Big Bruvver.'

Fred is keeping his distance because I stink like a septic tank.

'So what's on offer, Fred-ric? A 'oliday in Scotland? Or Butlin's at Clacton? I'd 'ave to learn t'swim, wooden'I?

'Alex, Alex. How terrible. I thought you were at the grammar school?'

'Yeah. A scholarship to Eton, is it? Fourteenth in my El-ec-ty-on, am I?' I grin, displaying a few stained teeth. '*She* wanted a nice clean little boykins, something small, neat and posh she could dress up and send to Eton.'

Fred doesn't follow. Lack of hed-ucation.

'So where's that famous "royalty", Fred, eh? "Out o' my own pocket," you says. You begged me, didn'ya? So I spoke to 'im, didn'ah? Poor Fred, bombed aht, do 'im a favour, guv. Forget Mr El-y-ot, old Fred's the raght stuff. Yeah.'

'Alex, I assure you, George brought me the manuscript entirely of his own volition.'

''Is what? Oh dooh tell mee, Fred-ric.'

Fred stammers his story about the pub off the Strand.

'So that's all raght then, i'n't?' I says. 'Nuffink t'do with yours truly. No re-ver-se cha-aarge phone cawl.' I tilt my throat back for what's left of the Worthington. 'Spell "socialism",' I tells 'im.

'What? Sell it?'

'S-p-p-pell it, cunt. Spell Whore-berg.'

He stands himself straight. 'You dare! You filthy little Nazi!' His last stand.

'Adolf 'ad only one ball. True or false?'

At this juncture – is that the word, *le mot juste*, as Fred would say? – who should come pedalling along but my old pal and village idiot, Tom Frederick. Not 'Fredric' but a proper English Frederick (though that might be German, you never know). Weaving-drunk.

''Ere, Tom!'

Tom's taking it all in, but not fast. Never fast, Tom. His eye is riveted by the Jag, then the gent, who's kind of melting into the chassis like Winston's mouth into Julia's.

'This is a foreigner, Tom, come to filch yer farm.'

'Uh?' (Tom.)

'Come to defile your muvver, Tom.'

'Uh?' Tom's eyes are crossed. Fred is easing his camel-hair arse into the driver's seat. I gets to him as the lovely engine purrs into life.

'So where's yer foreskin, then? Show us!'

Tom holds him down while I piss Worthington's on to his Trotsky Popular Front. Viva Franco! as the raped nun said. Heil Himmler all over his Westminster Abbey & Christ Church. We loot his fancy cigarette case, crocodile-skin wallet, keys, money. Business cards strewn in the mud. Me and Tom peering at them, cross-eyed, scratching our thatch wiv pitchforks, oohaah. The Jag's burning quietly.

'Tom,' says I, ''ave you ever been in a minhority of one – my son?'

'Wha'?' Tom guffaws, thinks it's something dirty out of *Spanking Stories* or *One Night in a Girls' School.*

'What ah mean, Tom,' I sez, 'is 'ave you ever stood alone, mate, alone against everyone, 'olding tight to *an unpopulhaar OPINION*!'

'Wha'?' sez Tom, a living compost heap.

'Because true courage, you arsehole, is not the boy who stood on the burning deck, is not the boy who fought for his farm in mid-winter, so who is it, eh?'

Tom grinning. 'Spitfire pilot, i'n't?'

'Haybag! True courage is the Lord Fauntleroy who rises in class in clean underpants to announce: "Sah, I doo nott beleeeve in h-h-anging! And, sah, I just lahv huns, wogs, coons, nigs, spivs, frogs, yids and pervs."'

'Nah ... ? Stone the crows. Whoahahoa ...'

'He doesn't have long, Alex,' Fred kept saying, as the Jag ate up the miles. 'George' was only forty-six – funny, I'd never attached an age to Eric. He was just somewhere up there. I felt sick and hollow with hunger; I wanted to climb out, anywhere. Fred was talking:

'He dreams of death now: splendid buildings, streets and ships, always bathed in sunlight.'

'Is it the TB? He told me he was "in the clear" on the TB.'

'You didn't know his first wife had died?'

I shook my head. Fred was quite keen on anything I didn't know about Eric.

'George was in Germany at the time,' Fred drawled. 'Soon after he sent you the postcard from Paris, Eileen had a woman's operation – her heart failed under the anaesthetic. Only thirty-nine and mother to an adopted baby boy. Terrible.'

'Is that the one Eric rescued from the sea?'

'Ay, yes, in Scotland. George was always insisting I should go up there, but it wasn't my cup of tea.'

'Eric wanted to adopt me but she wouldn't let him.'

It haunted him. But it was a joint decision they both made. They wanted someone much younger, someone as yet unformed, someone who wouldn't remember his real parents. Do you hold it against him?'

'Why should I? They probably decided I was the wrong sort.'

'Sort? Class, you mean?' Fred took both hands off the wheel – though he never drove with more than one, even at a hundred miles an hour – to make an eloquent gesture of denial (as he might have put it). 'Class! You can't mean class, Alex! Not with George!'

'He didn't think I was educated. I'd missed out on the eleven-plus to grammar school. I was your delinquent four days out of five. I was twelve. There was no way he could stuff me through Latin and into a public school by the age of thirteen.'

Fred changed the subject as adroitly as he moved the gears of his Jag. The rev counter spun, needles flipped all over the real-wood dashboard. The automatic cigar-lighter went click.

'So what's Eric's new wife like?' I asked.

'Beautiful, charming, efficient, a literary lady who knows *everyone*.'

'I see.' I could only imagine someone like Ellen.

'Maybe you *will* see her, Alex.'

'Ah.' Despondently I studied my disgusting school clothes again. Then Fred pitched into the subject of Eric and women, keenly monitoring my reactions with eyes rolling like radar screens. Fred turned the world into words as if that was the purpose of living. I kept my own eye on the road throughout.

'According to Cyril Connolly, George used to stuff his hands into the pockets of his Eton trousers and hint that he knew Soho inside out. One day he said to Cyril, "Your trouble is that you're not interested in sex." Cyril was deeply upset. He swore he was thinking about it all the time. George said much the same thing to Aldous Huxley, who was suffering agonies as a half-blind Eton master. "Your trouble, sir," said George to Huxley, "is that you're more interested in Utopia than in Eros." Well, that was more than poor Aldous could take. We all know the result, *Brave New World*, everyone unzipping for programmed copulation. But now George sneers at Aldous. "The more holy he gets," says George, "the more his books stink with sex." The real George, of course, is the character you find in those early novels published by Gollancz – going to elaborate pains to take his best girl for a country Sunday, then finding at the crucial moment that the ground is wet or he's a penny short of the return train fare. George not only expects the worst but – in my view – needs it. He was always sure that if he had children, Goering would target a flying bomb straight at the cradle.'

'He said he was sterile.'

'Ah. So he told you that, too. One day you should write it all down before your memory lapses. He's not allowing anyone to write his biography, you know. For George, all biographers are charlatans –'

'Like all publishers are swindlers.'

'Sometimes, Alex, you remind me of O'Brien, the man in Room 101. You like to display the caged rats, don't you?'

'A rat is nothing special on a farm.'

'Of course you had great charm five years ago. All that eagerness and innocence. I dare say George got too close to you and then felt he had to escape abroad as a war correspondent.'

'Is that what he told you?'

'George never examines his own sub-conscious. He thinks the sub-conscious is another Continental swindle. I sent him Sartre's book on anti-semitism, which I was proud to publish. I thought he'd admire Sartre's psychological categories but

George called him "a bag of wind" and promised to give him "a good boot". George distrusts abstract categories. He thinks philosophy should be forbidden by law. Big thoughts, Big Brother – no thought. George is the crown jewel of a peculiar English genius for embracing the lesser evil. That's what he means by "decent". One defeats the fanatic precisely by not being a fanatic oneself. Such is George's genius that he has turned the relative, the lesser evil, into an absolute for an entire generation.'

Fred reminded me of a bluebottle allowed to perch, undisturbed, on a large cut of beef.

'You don't look Jewish, Fred,' I said.

'I'm probably the first and only Jew you've set eyes on.'

I wanted to get out, go home. My dread was rising. When I asked for a fag, Fred looked quite shocked but he didn't argue. He'd probably have administered opium if that was what it took to get me to the hospital. But not food, because that meant stopping.

As soon as the Jag entered the streets of London I felt my bile coming up. There were coloured faces everywhere and the girls looked like tarts. The restaurants were mostly foreign. Swindlers, spivs and bohemians lounging at street-corners. I wondered whether this was where Eric really belonged when he wasn't striding 'down' our way with his haversack, his big boots and his shooting stick.

Fred pointed out several special cars, as if to humour me, including a 1936 Riley Lynx 1½-litre sports tourer. 'Cost you over four hundred pounds,' Fred warned, as if I might be on the brink of leaping out and buying it. 'And that's the new Daimler. And this is UCH.'

We had come to rest outside a massive building, hundreds

of windows, University College Hospital. My hand was shaking. I'd never known such panic. Fred was talking all the time. 'One of London's great teaching hospitals ... I know the surgeon here ... first-class ... I had George transferred ... I, I, I.'

The crocodile-skin wallet appeared, five pounds in my hand.

'Aren't you coming in, then?' I protested.

'George wants to see you alone. He was emphatic about it. By the way: if you meet the new wife in there, don't mention that you possess "The Willow Tree".'

'Why?'

'She'll want it. She will rule the George Orwell Estate with a rod of iron.'

'Does that mean you want it?'

'For safekeeping.'

'Where's my "scout's royalty", then?'

Fred sighed as if he'd been fending off crooks all his life.

'I've just given you five pounds.'

'I thought that was for the fare home. Plus something to eat.'

'All of which could cost you a pound at the most. If you send me "The Willow Tree" you shall receive a cheque for a further five pounds.'

Reluctantly I climbed out. Fred was extracting a poshly wrapped gift-box from the boot.

'It's yours to give. Pamela chose it. She adores George. We had Thomas Mann here recently, I've published him and his brother Heinrich for years. I gave a lunch party at the Carlton for Tommy, twenty-four guests ...'

A cold wind was bouncing off the cliff-face of the hospital. Somewhere up there, behind one of those the-same windows, was Eric. The Ministry of Love, I remembered, had no windows. Fred was rattling on:

'Mann engaged in earnest conversation with Ernest Newman about Schönberg and atonal music. Pamela was sitting the other side of him, out of the conversation – except for Mann's hand resting on her thigh above her stockings. It's the duality of flesh and spirit, you see.'

Finally Fred stopped. The wind wormed inside my worn black blazer. I think Fred understood and shared my fear. His hand was tremulous as it warmly gripped mine.

'Alex, you will find a mutual friend with a translucent skin and a furnace burning beneath. His hair has thinned and turned white. But nothing can infect his spirit. Good luck.'

He handed me his business card then the Jag was lost in the traffic. I walked through the main door – VISITORS – clutching the posh parcel. I'd been too shaken to ask what it was 'I' was supposed to be giving Eric. I only knew I was to ask for Room 101.

CHAPTER XII

At the reception desk the female clerk refused to accord me a glance for five minutes. She wore a bun beneath a starched white cap and used a voice like tinkling Crown Derby to put the world in its place. An appointment was granted as a favour, but all favours were provisional: 'We'll have to see how he is tomorrow, won't we?'

I was in a state of shock. Getting out of bed that morning I'd examined the grime on the inside of my shirt collar and decided it would do one more day. I'd walked to school shoving small kids from the elementary school into the gutter, as normal. And here I was in London, hollow with hunger, clutching a ridiculous, fancy box and already wondering whether I could save Fred's fiver by hitch-hiking home. I'd be dumb not to try.

I cleared my throat. 'Excuse me, miss.'

Slowly her pale blue eyes settled on me. Did I have an appointment? Evidently not. She couldn't find my name in the book. Evidently I was a liar. When I suggested she look under Fred's name, she surveyed me like a slug on a lettuce leaf.

'How do you spell that?'

My head spun. 'W-h ... W-a-r-b-e-r-g.'

'You mean "u".'

Yew mean yew. I hadn't heard an accent like that since Ellen Cripps said 'Scum like you should be in Borstal', though she hadn't said anything of the sort, because I never did work for Cripps, Reverend Goodfellow having got me a free place at the grammar school since my maths was so good and because I'd saved his life from Jessie and Bluebell, though only in a dream. I was never in Borstal and when I wrote my letter to Eric I was only feigning illiteracy, just for fun. I hope that affords you a clear and coherent view, m'dear.

Five more minutes of third-degree by the receptionist followed. This was definitely the same woman who did or didn't horse-whip Eric for wetting his prep-school bed. I suddenly remembered Eric's own tale of his time in a Paris hospital for the poor. He had been suffering from pneumonia. To reach the ward he'd been forced to walk for some two hundred yards along a frosty gravel path, with the wind whipping his nightshirt round his bare calves. He'd been put in a ward with sixty other paupers, the beds almost touching, and then subjected to a series of disgusting assaults by doctors and students who never spoke to him or looked him in the eye. It had reminded him of a story he'd heard as a child; and I was now reminded of his story.

The only thing in my favour was Fred's spectacular gift-box. Finally a suspicious nurse led me along corridors smelling of antiseptic and linoleum polish. Was this the odour that Eric had encountered in the Paris hospital, which he called 'foul, faecal yet sweetish'? I half expected to find him in a public ward, being force-fed on thin vegetable soup with slimy hunks of bread floating about in it. We kept passing old people on trolleys.

We now entered a private wing of the hospital. You could tell. There was a carpet instead of linoleum, and the paint was fresher. Instead of large wards you had a series of private rooms with individual name plates. Everything was quieter, wrapped in hush. Eventually the nurse paused outside a door and gestured to me to stand still and be silent (as if I'd been singing lewd songs at the top of my voice). She went inside, firmly closing the door behind her. No peeping here.

Room 101.

When she came out she was carrying a bedpan. I remembered Eric heading for the bog in the Crown Hotel after inventing the story of Gulliver's gigantic crap.

'Mr Blay-er is sleeping. You had better come back tomorrow.'

'I'll wait, then.'

'Well, you can't wait here.'

I had a feeling that if I ever went downstairs I'd never get back up again because of the third-degree and the 'I haven't got all day' attitude at the reception desk. The nurse obviously didn't think I was the sort who should be visiting Mr Blair, the smart literary people who put their paws up ladies' thighs while chattering about Schnitzler or whoever it was. Her eyes told me that my black blazer and grey flannels should have been at the dry cleaner's. And didn't I realise that clothes-rationing had now ended – everything 'coupon-free' (but not money-free, my old bag). So I just put the gift-box on the floor, dug my hands in my pockets and leaned back against the wall in the kind of menacing slouch I used to adopt in the school corridor when planning to give Joe Pilkington or Tom Frederick the full works.

The nurse was about to let me have an earful when another, prettier nurse bustled up, a bit like Vivien Leigh, I thought, pushing a trolley laden with dishes of food covered by silvery lids. She gave me a smashing smile. She was definitely human. Matthews to Carter to Lawton, it's a goal! My stomach heaved at the smell of cooked food.

'He'll be awake in half a trice. Loves his food, does Mr Blay-er.'

Eric's was quite a small room but comfortable. There were vases of flowers and bowls of fruit and piles of books and magazines. His face was like transparent wax and completely hollowed out. His mouth hung open. His breathing sounded like a chain-saw running down. I wondered whether he was dreaming his death-dreams, of sunlit buildings and ships. I hung in the doorway while Vivien Leigh gently coaxed him out of sleep, hauled him upright and propped big pillows behind his back. His haggard features were creased with pain as she pulled him up.

Eric gazed intently at his food, which she'd placed on a special bed-tray. He didn't notice me. He was three-quarters asleep. He looked a bit drugged, too.

'You've got a young visitor, Mr Blay-er!'

I took a step or two into the room.

His eyes lay deep in dark sockets. They didn't focus beyond the food. Slowly, with the careful deliberation I remembered, he began to eat. I noticed the missing fingernails.

'Why don't you just sit yourself down while he's eating,' Vivien Leigh whispered in my ear. 'It takes him a while to properly wake up.' She smelt lovely.

I sat down with Fred's gift on my knee. The nurse went out, closing the door. Eric's interest was squarely focused on two slices of roast beef, two roast potatoes, and a hunk of Yorkshire pudding.

We always have good roast beef and Yorkshire pudding on Sundays.

Eileen makes the best pastry in London. You like roast beef, don't you?

Yes!

With the potatoes roasted under the joint so that the juices seep into them.

Eric was chewing slowly, as if his jaws ached, or he feared they might, and his adam's apple seemed enormous in his thin, scarred neck as he swallowed. I felt sick with hunger.

'So you thought *Nineteen Eighty-Four* was a bit "over the top", did you?' Eric said, still intent on his food. 'Too much "gloom and doom", eh?'

I sat rigid and mute. My heart was pounding.

'I got married recently,' Eric said. 'In this room. David fixed it with the Archbishop of Canterbury. Anthony and Malcolm found me a posh velvet smoking jacket for the occasion. The bride and the guests went off to celebrate in the Ritz, and I was allowed to listen to the radio in bed. They brought me the signed menu.'

But he didn't say all this in one go. It came in wispy threads, punctuated by slow, grinding chewing. Then he'd pick up the thread again. His eyes remained fixed on the tray throughout.

'So how long has it been, Winston?'

'Alex.'

'Alex. What did I call you?'

'It's been five years, six months and three days.'

At this he looked up, gazed at me, then smiled faintly.

'You were always the one who could do his sums. Still at the grammar school, are you?'

'I'm taking the School Certificate this summer.'

'What about the English master who offered you five quid for your copy of *Animal Farm*?'

'Boothroyd.'

'Boothroyd. Did you accept his offer?'

I shook my head.

'Hm. Well, English was scarcely a subject in my day. It was supposed to be covered by Latin and Greek, you see. But you haven't done Latin?'

'No.'

'So what next?'

My head hung down. 'Certain gents you may remember have offered me part-time mucking out on their farms.'

Eric stopped chewing for a moment. 'That's no good, is it?'

I nodded. 'I'd like to try for agricultural college, but – '

Eric was having a hard time with a roast potato which kept slithering about his plate. In the course of the battle he was splashing his sheet with gravy.

'Want any help?' I asked.

'How much would it cost?'

'What?'

'Agricultural college.'

I shrugged. 'No idea. I've got this present for you from Fred.'

'Put it down somewhere. Probably from Pamela. More fancy pyjamas or a Dali.'

I placed it on the floor near his bedside table. It seemed odd to be so near to Eric after all these years. At closer quarters there was a medical smell coming off him.

'I have some money now,' he said. 'Damn. Yes, cut this bloody potato for me. It's odd how the body retains its hungers while perishing. One always gets money when one can no longer use it. Not that my beautiful bride stinted when she went out to choose herself an engagement ring. I modelled Julia on her in *Nineteen Forty-Eight*, you see. They're both fond of the word "Rubbish!"'

'*Eighty-Four*, Eric.'

'I told her what I've told every woman I've proposed to since Eileen died. "You're marrying a corpse and a secure income for life." That might sound attractive enough, but three out of four turned me down. She's very beautiful, you know. When she saw I was really going to die she said yes. There's a cheque book in the drawer.'

Slowly he went through some kind of soft custard pudding which looked quite good. I had begun to eye the boxes of biscuits and bowls of fruit beside his bed.

'Have a chocolate biscuit,' he said. 'Have two. We shared some strange meals in our time, I remember.'

'Thanks.' I leapt up. 'You used to drink your vile black tea out of a saucer,' I said. I took two chocolate biscuits, then another, then slipped the third one back into the packet, a bit thumbprinted.

'Daren't drink out of a saucer here. Posh place.'

'Better than that Paris hospital you told me about.'

'Every way better except in one respect – I left that one alive.' Carefully he lifted another dollop of custard pudding, pushing the spoon deep into his mouth, his wasted jaw fastening on it like a clamp.

'By the way, Eric,' I said.

'Hmm?'

'It's not true about Swift flinching from sending Gulliver to the bog.'

The spoon came out, licked clean. I couldn't read his expression: he might have understood, he might not. I pressed on:

'When we went to tea that day at the Crown Hotel, you

made up a long passage from *Gulliver* – beginning: "So urgent were my discomforts according to the promptings of nature ..." Then Gulliver couldn't help himself and ...'

'He farted?'

I moved a fraction closer to Eric's bed.

'"Whereupon my bowels, like slaves driven beyond obedience by desperation, let out an enormous explosion, the noise and odour of which caused all but his Majesty to fall to the ground."'

'I don't recall the passage,' Eric said. 'It doesn't sound like Swift.' He looked doubly drained by the effort. 'The memory goes.'

'No, Eric, I told you – you made up the passage. You said Swift had flinched from sending Gulliver to the bog. But my English master –'

'Boothroyd.'

'Boothroyd pointed out to me that Swift doesn't flinch.'

'Congratulate Boothroyd for me.'

'He showed me the real passage. "I had been for some hours extremely pressed by the necessities of nature ... it being almost two days since I had last disburthened myself."'

Eric chuckled. '"Disburthened" is quite good. Did I make that up?'

'No, that's Swift.'

'Ah.'

'So Gulliver crept into his tiny house "and discharged my body of that uneasy load".'

Eric chuckled again. '"Uneasy" – excellent.'

'Later Gulliver made a practice of performing "that business" in the open air, with two servants carting off the "offensive matter" in wheelbarrows.'

'I must have overlooked this gallant mucking out of

mountainous ordure. Or perhaps I was showing off. Or do you think it was more sinister than that – a straight swindle?'

'When I told Boothroyd –'

'Ah. Boothroyd.'

'He said I must have got it wrong because you could never make a mistake like that. Boothroyd told me you'd read *Gulliver* half a dozen times.'

'I think we both have to bow to Boothroyd.'

I was now regretting having raised the subject, I don't know why I did, I think I was just teasing Eric and proving how much I remembered of what he'd said. But I could see he wasn't taking it too well. Then I noticed the fishing rods poking from beneath the bed. He said he was taking them to a Swiss sanatorium.

'I hope you find a willow tree,' I said.

He smiled. He didn't miss anything.

Eric had finished his lunch. He tried to push the tray away. I put it lower down the bed. He was struggling in some discomfort. There was no flesh on him at all. From his sighs I could tell he was suffering from bed sores. His left arm reached out towards the bedside cabinet but he couldn't steady his hand and he sank back into the pillows with a groan.

'How's that farm of yours?' he said faintly.

'It belongs to Colonel Cripps.'

'Wasn't that the one with a daughter called Mollie?'

'Ellen.'

'You should be careful with that type of girl. They make havoc then run off with some Yank. What about the animal rebellion? How did Cripps put it down? Buckshot?

'There was no animal rebellion.'

'I expect not. Did you ever get that chapter I sent you? "The Last Man."'

'"The Willow Tree."'

'I destroyed it. Too reactionary.'

'I didn't understand all of it. But I enjoyed Benjamin the donkey's "Which page are we on?"'

Eric looked tired – I could tell he didn't remember.

'I suppose Fred dragged you up to London.'

'I'm glad to see you, Eric. I'm sorry you're ill.'

'Your voice hadn't broken in those days, of course. Not yet the big, shy youth who now walks in, cloaked in caution, the armoured Ironside. Small boys have a special charm, I suppose. I didn't do very well by you, did I? Write the cheque out. I can sign it. Pay Winston Smith Esquire five hundred pounds.'

'Alex Jones.'

'Deposit it in Post Office Savings, that's the best place. I always liked post offices.'

'There's no need,' I mumbled, desperate for the money.

'Of course my wife will have to live her own life. There isn't a famous painter or philosopher in Europe she hasn't had an affair with, so that shouldn't be a difficulty. It's odd, really: we first did it some years ago, when she was still saying no to marriage, and now it's legal and there's nothing I can do about it. Not that illness kills desire, you see. I often think that one may experience an agonising sexual urge for several seconds after death. What do you think of that? How does that idea strike you? I may have picked it up from Dali, he's quite a good draughtsman but otherwise disgusting. Whereas Picasso has a conscience of sorts. So when will they drop the hydrogen bomb, do you think?'

'More "gloom and doom",' I said. 'By the way, if as many

atomic bombs had been tossed around as you indicate in *Nineteen Eighty-Four*, the earth would have been too contaminated to sustain human life thirty years later.'

'Hm.'

'Tell me about your young son, Eric. How old is he?'

'Three. No, five. He was three when the boat capsized. I thought we were goners. I should never have taken him in the boat.'

'Why did you go looking for puffins' eggs?'

'A tendency to regard myself as Gulliver – more accurately, Robinson Crusoe. It was later pointed out to me that we'd just had breakfast and were hardly likely to spend a year on the island.'

'A bit like when Sergeant Blair forgot to hammer the Home Guard spigot mortar into the ground?'

'What? Did I tell you that?'

'Fred did.'

'Don't believe a word he says. What's wrong with a spot of concussion or a new denture, anyway? If someone offered to knock all my teeth out in return for ten more years, I'd call it a bargain. In fact I'd settle for three provided I was granted the strength to write. But the doctors aren't saying, you see, so I know which page I'm on.'

'Like Benjamin the donkey?'

Eric smiled faintly. He still didn't remember what he'd written.

'My son will remember me as the dad who was always lying down and couldn't play. He used to come to me and ask, "Where have you hurt yourself?" He lives with my sister now. She lets him play with his thingummy. That's essential, you see. Otherwise it's premature ejaculation all through your life. I always suspected that my mother and nanny didn't allow me to play with my thingummy. I once plucked up courage to ask my nurse in later life whether I'd been allowed to fiddle with my willy in the bath, but she was very deaf and replied, "Oh yes, and you kept throwing it out on to the floor." It's a pity about my son. We no sooner had him than Eileen died. And then I took a cigarette end to his adoption certificate and burned a hole where the names of his real parents were given. That wasn't a reasonable thing to do. I don't suppose he'll forgive me when he sees it. He'll think I wasn't a reasonable person. I could never have done that with you, Alex, you always knew who your real dad was.'

'I was the wrong sort for you. And your wife.'

He winced. A large foot suddenly protruded at the end of the bed. Some pain was shooting through him. Most of his toenails had gone. He reached for the bell. V. Leigh hurried in with some tablets and an injection. I watched her roll up his pyjama sleeve. The arm was a stick. He groaned as the needle found a slither of flesh. His face was haggard, his eyes sunken.

'Now this young man isn't tiring you, is he, Mr Blay-er?'

'Not at all,' Eric whispered. 'An old friend, you see.'

'Isn't that a lovely present he's brought? Aren't we going to unwrap it?'

'No.'

She took up the food tray and hustled out.

'Of course,' he said, 'one can overdo the charms of childhood. There's a poem by Thomas Hood. Do you know him?'

I shook my head.

'It's a poem about trying to describe the beauties of childhood, but he can't get on with his writing because his children are making too much noise. "Go to your mother, child, and blow your nose."'

I slipped myself another chocolate biscuit.

'You missed your lunch,' he said. 'Fred promised to find you a sandwich in a pub but he never found a pub. Loves his new car too much to climb out. Take the whole packet. I'll call the nurse and order you a proper dinner.'

'Please don't bother, these are fine.'

'I want to be buried by Church of England rites, it's in my will,' Eric said. 'Preferably a graveyard in the Thames valley, with the waters flowing sluggishly by. "HERE LIES ERIC ARTHUR BLAIR, BORN 25 JUNE 1903, DIED – What's your guess on that, Alex?'

'My guess is that Mr Blair will outlive Dr Orwell.'

'Hm. I planted that idea on you: Halloween '43, wasn't it? Dr Jekyll and Mr Hyde. And later Mr B. and Dr O. With you nothing ever failed to take root. You're damning me for being a rich and famous writer, aren't you?'

'No, why should I?'

'Because someone else befriended you – not me. I tried to warn you.'

'Writers are foxes, you said.'

'How's that cheque? Alex Jones Esquire, one thousand pounds.'

'You said five hundred.'

'I've never admired a boy so much as you.'

'You went away and you took care never to send an address.'

'You must stay and meet my wife. I always liked post offices. There was one attached to the village store in Wallington before Eileen and I loved there. I mean lived there. No electricity, no hot water from the tap and a primitive contraption in the back garden. The cottage used to belong to a firm called Agrar before our time. They had a model farm there, too, one of those experimental places. It was called Manor Farm. I remember using the name in my book. You pick up names where you can.'

I now had his cheque book on my lap. I had unscrewed the cap of my fountain pen, shoved it on the back of the stem, and licked the nib.

'Manor Farm was our farm,' I said.

'Yes, they had to close it down during the Depression,' Eric said. 'It stuck in my head. I used it in the book. I called Wallington something else, though.'

'You called it Willingdon,' I said. 'But that was really our village, Porterstone.' My voice was rising. Eric was wiping out the Joneses all over again.

He sank deeper into his pillows.

'How are those two boys you always pretended you didn't like?'

'Joe and Tom, you mean?'

'Ah yes, Joe and Tom. That was a cold winter.'

'Joe Pilkington was sent off to his posh school with his curls smarmed down and a gleaming tuck box. Tom Frederick has just about learned to write his own name.'

'They took it all away from you, didn't they?'

Eric began coughing badly and the young nurse hurried in again. The coughing wouldn't stop. His suffering was terrible. Do it to Julia, don't do it to me. Helpless, even the nice nurse turned against me.

'Mrs Blay-er is due shortly and we don't want him poorly when she comes, do we?'

Eric tried to protest against my expulsion but it only made his coughing worse. She held a bowl under his chin and I was reminded of how he and I had struggled to save dying lambs. He was clutching his chest while making futile gestures with the other hand, as if urging me to sit down and stay. But his voice had gone. The waters were carrying us apart for ever. He made a huge effort and waved me to take a sheet of paper sitting on his bedside table. It was a letter addressed to me.

I'd written out the cheque by now, enough money to change my life, but I had too much pride to press it into his shaking hand, with the nurse watching. I left Room 101 and found my way out of the building, into unknown streets, asking the way like a foreigner. There would be no agricultural college, just slaving for Cripps, Pilkington and Frederick. It took me all night to hitch back to Porterstone but I saved Fred's fiver. I read Eric's letter in a lorry drivers' café while waiting for my fourth lift. It was dated 3 Oct. 1949 and was written on both sides of a sheet of lined paper torn from a rough pad.

Dear Alex,

I keep meaning to write to you, but each time I make the attempt I run out of steam. It's my lungs. I'm hoping to travel to a sanatorium in Switzerland soon. They say it will do me good. Sorry about my handwriting. They have taken my typewriter away.

The future lies with your generation. Your first responsibility is to preserve the integrity of our language. It's the finest in the world but increasingly debased by jargon, evasive euphemism, and phrases tacked together like the sections of a pre-fabricated hen-house. Short, Saxon words are usually the best, I find.

The real question is whether the people who wipe their

boots on us during the next fifty years are to be called managers, bureaucrats or politicians. The question is whether capitalism, now obviously doomed, is to give way to oligarchy, or to true democracy. I do not regard a small farm, incidentally, as 'capitalism'. It's earning a living, which is a different kettle of fish. How's that big barn of yours? Is Boxer still alive? I have forgotten the name of his mare. Was it Mollie?

[Line crossed out.]

I regard you as English yeoman stock. You defend your own without fear or favour. You have also inherited a basic decency which has held our nation together for centuries. I was glad that my novel 1984 reached you safely. I expect you're right and I did go a bit 'over the top'. You almost certainly did not notice that my main character resembles the man I believe you will grow up to be. Anyway, the novel was meant to be a warning, not a prophecy.

I do not believe that history has to be a series of swindles (although it usually has been) foisted on a brainless mob whose destiny is always to be led or driven, as one gets a pig back to the sty by kicking it on the bottom or rattling a stick inside a swill-bucket. I think we human beings can choose our own fate. To some extent, anyway.

[Three lines crossed out.]

It still seems to me that Democratic Socialism is our best hope of putting decency on an organised basis. You probably [crossed out]. They took away my typewriter. Without it I [crossed out]

I doubt whether any of the above makes much sense. It's the usual tiredness. I used to say to you that a writer with a hook [*sic*] in his head is not going to die until it gets written. I have two or three books in my head but one's luck has to run out some time. So [crossed out]

So [crossed out]

There will always be some individuals like yourself who [crossed out]

Some twenty years after Eric's death I received a somewhat impertinent letter. It arrived while I was in France negotiating the weekly sale of two thousand lambs for fattening, most of them raised on my Welsh hill farms. I have already told you how on that occasion I was taken to lunch as only the French can lunch, having visited Chartres and discovered Eric carved on every saintly façade. My principal investment was now in three thousand acres south of Cambridge. The truth is that the arable land around Porterstone is of mediocre quality, and when I bought out Pilkington and Frederick in fairly rapid succession I pulled down the hedges and created a safari park, with a good access road from the new motorway. I gave Joe a trial run on the promotion and merchandising side but these days you need more than charm and a gift for driving new Land Rovers into old trees. As for Tom, he will continue to feed my big predators without fear until he turns his back once too often.

You may wonder, reader, how I had so picked myself up out of misfortune. The answer must lie beyond these pages but I can hint at it modestly enough: the spirit of the age, the recovery of Enterprise. It was Fred, incidentally, who put me through agricultural college, though I never gave him 'The Willow Tree' – a very decent English gent, as it turned out.

When Cripps died I was able to pick up Manor Farm for a song; the colonel's death duties and debts dominated my brief negotiation with the twice-divorced Ellen, who entertained the fanciful hope of remaining in residence at a nominal rent. Apart from restoring the farmhouse for my mother, with a maid living in, I created an Animal Fun Farm for children, with retired cart-horses and donkeys, the heirs of Boxer, Clover and Benjamin, providing safe transport.

I hope this little memoir will raise our profile. Most popular are the uncannily lifelike waxwork models of Eric Blair talking to the pigs, drinking tea from his saucer, and saving Boxer from Knacker Simmonds. There is a 50p additional charge for a view of 'The Willow Tree' manuscript in its special showcase, half-price for children.

It was this that no doubt prompted the impertinent letter, already mentioned, which I received shortly after we opened. The new George Orwell Archive requested permission to submit the typescript of 'The Willow Tree' to scholarly examination. No carbon copy had ever been traced; there was some evidence that Mr Orwell may have destroyed it; and I was frankly advised that certain 'experts' were of the opinion that he had never written it. The word 'forgery' was not used but it fairly hummed between the lines.

I leave it for the interested reader to judge, now that my story is finished – just as Mr Orwell himself appended his 'Principles of Newspeak' to *Nineteen Eighty-Four.*

I duly wrote back to the George Orwell Archive under the letterhead of Alex Jones Holdings, plc, Berkeley Square, as follows:

Dear Sirs,

Which page are we on, comrades? No page.

Yours sincerely,

Benjamin the donkey.

APPENDIX

THE LAST MAN [deleted] THE WILLOW TREE
by George Orwell

The boy lay down under the willow tree beside the pond. He intended to read the book he was carrying in his old fishing bag but it was a warm summer day with gnats hovering above the muddy water and he soon fell into a reverie. Winston Jones [deleted] Smith was twelve [deleted] fourteen years old. This farm, with its long, rolling pasture, had recently belonged to his family, but various misfortunes had forced them to sell, and now there was a new owner. He was a decent enough man who partly understood the boy's feelings and let him muck about on the farm at weekends; but the boy was no longer invited into the farmhouse, which had been his home since he was born.

The truth was that the new owner did not want to understand Winston's real feelings. Probably the boy himself could not have explained them. He had the thoughts but not the words. A family farm is more than a home, and more than a way of earning a living. It is a way of life. Winston had once dared to mention to the new owner that some of the older animals, the ones with names, and most of the dogs, were no longer happy about their treatment. Not that the new owner was cruel, he simply had his own ways of doing things which were not those to which the animals (and Winston) were accustomed.

But the new owner indicated fairly sharply that he needed no advice from a mere boy, and after that Winston kept his thoughts to himself, consoling his old friends, the aggrieved dogs and horses, when the man's back was turned.

Winston's eyes began to close beneath the willow tree. His right arm crooked itself into a pillow beneath his head. The book, which described a rebellion by farm animals against human rule, slipped from his fingers into the long grass. He had already read most of it and only one or two chapters remained. It was a fairy story, really, although obviously written for adults as well as children. Winston had known the author, who used to visit the farm when it was half abandoned. The boy couldn't quite make up his mind whether he sympathised with the animal rebellion or he didn't. As a farmer's son he knew that farm animals could never survive without human protection and human skills. Even so, he agreed that the regular slaughter of pigs, chicken and lambs was not necessarily what those creatures would have chosen for themselves.

An old cart-horse called Boxer was grazing in the meadow not many yards from the willow tree. Boxer was very fond of Winston. Presently he ambled across to nudge the boy with his white-striped nose, to make sure he was asleep and not dead. Winston stirred and Boxer, satisfied, delicately picked up the book between his chompers and slowly carried it up to the pigsties where he respectfully laid it before the revered champion boar, old Major. All the boars were sleeping, but in the sties adjacent to old Major's the two most powerful and intelligent, Napoleon and Snowball, each opened an eye.

If Boxer had been asked why he did this he would probably have replied that Winston wanted him to do it, although Winston hadn't exactly said so. Boxer had spent much of his life understanding, and usually obeying, the boy's wishes. Boxer could not have put this into words but the understanding between the boy and the horse was more real than any words.

After the pigs read the book, the word spread and all the animals rose in rebellion against the owner of the farm and chased him out. This done, they held a meeting and gravely debated whether Winston should be allowed on the farm, even though he walked on two legs. Each animal had his own point of view about this. For Boxer and his mare Clover, the boy was a trusted friend and no more need be said. Some of the dogs wondered where their biscuits would come from if Winston, too, was chased out. As for the ambitious boars, Napoleon and Snowball, each had his own reason for getting rid of the boy, but as soon as the one heard the other's reason he had second thoughts. Napoleon in particular had a number of second and third thoughts which finally added up, or subtracted down, to:

'Let him stay for the time being.'

Napoleon's acolyte Squealer promptly rushed round the farm carrying the message. The cart-horse Boxer, meanwhile, dutifully plodded down the pasture to wake Winston up – the boy had slept through the entire Animal Rebellion.

'Napoleon says you can stay.' Boxer hesitated. 'For the time being.'

Napoleon rapidly decided that the other farm animals could

not be trusted to understand the book without 'revolutionary guidance'. Napoleon assigned the task to Squealer. His tail whisking with excitement, Squealer was soon reading out selected extracts from the book to packed meetings of the animals.

Snowball was busy making speeches and organising committees, while Napoleon concentrated on training his dogs in the loft above the harness room. It was a strange time, as bits and pieces of the human language began to fall out of unlikely mouths. The boy's main concerns were what they had always been: repairing hedges and milking cows. He was also learning how to get the tractor and thresher, which had been sabotaged during the Rebellion, back into action. There came the day when all the animals lined up to watch Winston drive the tractor for the first time. Snowball was observing him with intense concentration, trying to figure out how a pig could do it. Only Napoleon absented himself from the ceremony.

One day Squealer summoned Winston to the barn, where the boy found him in the shadows, half hidden in straw, only his snout and the tip of his restless tail visible.

'We urgently need a line on the book. Must have a line. Comrade Napoleon is insisting on a line. A line.'

'A line?'

'Must have a line. Comrade Napoleon says only the early chapters in the book are true.'

'Ah – the Rebellion, you mean?'

'Correct. But Comrade Snowball says the later chapters may also be true.'

'Ah – the Repression, you mean?'

'Comrade Snowball says the later chapters will be true unless we eliminate Comrade Napoleon.' Squealer's tail whisked in agitation. 'That's where you come in – Comrade Chairman Napoleon says.'

'Why me?' Winston asked.

'You knew the author. You must explain why he wrote some true chapters and some false chapters.'

Winston thought about this. 'I think there may be a solution.'

'Yes!'

'The first chapters of the book were written by a friend of mine called Mr B. He used to visit the farm.'

'Yes, yes, we remember him.'

'But then Mr B. died and the rest of his book was written by a man called Dr O., who claimed he'd written it all himself.'

'Ah! And this Dr O. is an agent of Wall Street?'

'What's that?'

'World imperialism has its sty in Wall Street. It's a fact. This Dr O. is a lackey and running dog of imperialism.' Squealer hastily corrected himself. 'Running man. That's the line!'

That same day, at Napoleon's command, Squealer convened all the animals in the barn. Winston was instructed to attend. He wasn't allowed on the platform with the pigs; Squealer fussed and frothed about where exactly the boy should stand. Boxer and Clover arrived together, slow and weary, setting down their hairy hoofs with care lest there should be some small animal concealed in the straw. Clover looked happy and lifted her nose in Winston's direction; she was now a grandmother who had recently produced her own fifth foal. Then came Muriel, the white goat, and Benjamin the donkey, the oldest animal on the farm and a confirmed cynic.

Squealer beckoned all the animals to rise as the Comrade Chairman made his entrance, three fierce dogs at his heel. Winston noticed the low growls they directed at Snowball; for a moment the boy thought the big boar was destined for a savage exit ahead of schedule.

Squealer began his speech, skipping about the platform with his round cheeks and twinkling eyes, whisking his tail persuasively. He explained that the book had been written by two authors, one progressive, the other reactionary. Mr B., he continued, was a noble friend of animals, whereas Dr O. had grown rich on his own 'poisonous spittle'. The animals tried to absorb all this. Clearly they didn't understand.

Squealer sensed as much. He must have heard the cynical snort from Benjamin. Napoleon certainly did – his slits flashed their red warning. Squealer then bounded across the platform to Winston.

'Comrade, do your revolutionary duty and tell the meeting that every word written by your friend Mr B. is true and every word written by his sworn enemy, Dr O., is false.'

Rows of expectant, trusting, yet uncertain eyes were focused on the boy. He merely nodded – it seemed the best thing to do.

'A nod is as good as a wink,' Benjamin scoffed.

Squealer now produced his master card, something that all the animals could understand:

'Comrades, we now know where Mr B. ends and Dr O. begins. You are not to believe anything in the book after page ...'

But here Napoleon grunted extremely loudly, stopping Squealer in mid-sentence.

'We shall see,' Napoleon said.

'After page we shall see,' Squealer added quickly. Leaping

about on the platform, his tail coiled in knots of excitement, Commissar Squealer revealed that the later chapters of the book, that is to say those following page 'we shall see', had been serialised in the *Slaughterhouse Gazette*, pictorialised in the magazine *Man*, broadcast by the 'Voice of Two Legs', and translated into thirty human languages by the 'Estates Department'.

The dutiful animals, led by the cart-horses Boxer and Clover, the goat Muriel, and the sheep, chanted 'We shall see!' for the next ten minutes.

Snowball could take no more of it: 'Comrades, we must struggle against this counter-revolutionary "we shall see"!' But only the most intelligent of the animals properly understood him and the chanting and bleating continued.

'We shall see what we shall see,' grunted Napoleon as his snarling dogs forced a wide path for his exit.

It was all strangely familiar to Winston, yet somehow different. The animals in *Animal Farm* had begun in a state of perfect innocence, but here in the barn they were all looking over their shoulders before they started. The Rebellion was already old as soon as it was young; Napoleon, Snowball and Squealer were creatures grasping a revealed destiny, hardened revolutionaries returning from the long exile of human rule to settle accounts.

Snowball's behaviour towards Winston became increasingly belligerent. The boy was constantly being waylaid when going about his work by one or other of Snowball's 'toilers' committees'. Working on the tractor, supervising the cleaning of the stables, attempting to put Boxer or Clover in harness (which they now refused), Winston was likely to be interrupted by one of Snowball's delegations complaining about his human attitude – which they called 'false consciousness'. But at the first whiff of Napoleon's dogs the committees scattered on trotter, hoof, claw or wing.

Snowball himself began to invite Winston to secret rendezvous in the spinney or in the shadows of the ruined windmill. On one occasion the boy came across him hidden behind bales of straw in the barn, a ball-tipped pen clutched between the two knuckles of his trotters, slowly and painfully writing out passages from *Animal Farm* while grunting to himself in an effort to pronounce the harder words. He wanted to know, for example, what 'indefatigable' meant – because according to the book he, Snowball, was 'indefatigable' at organising animal committees.

'Yes, you are,' Winston assured him.

'But what does it mean, comrade?'

The boy wasn't sure himself but he knew better than to show doubt or hesitation in front of an animal. He said it meant 'clever' and continued to eat from his packet of potato crisps. Snowball looked a bit disappointed.

'Is that all it means?'

'It means you can't be defeated.'

At this the boar brightened and asked for a crisp. A Mars Bar was sticking out of Winston's pocket and he had his eye on that, too. According to the book, the birds on the farm did not understand Snowball's long words, but in reality – Snowball now confided – nor did Snowball.

'What does m-a-n-i-p-u-l-a-t-i-o-n mean?' he asked humbly.

'It might mean that animals should use their paws, trotters, hoofs and claws like human hands.'

Snowball frowned and sighed. 'But why must animals imitate humans in order to free themselves from human domination?'

'Oh, they must, comrade.'

Slowly Snowball turned the muddy pages of the book until he came to page 33. He began to read:

'"Now if there was one thing that the animals were completely certain of, it was that they did not want Jones back."' Snowball looked up. 'But what do we have now? We have half of Jones back. Yes, comrade. And half of Jones is likely to grow into the whole of Jones – in the course of time. I have been thinking, you see. Ownership isn't everything: management is your game. You're waiting until the animals have lost their way, until they can no longer do anything for themselves – and then back you'll come with your guns, whips, traps and harnesses.'

[*NOTE. Eric had deleted each 'Jones' and replaced it with 'Smith'.*]

Winston tossed him the Mars Bar. The pig fell upon it. Suddenly his tone was meek and pathetic:

'Comrade Winston, on what page does Mr B. end and Dr O. begin? Which of them wrote page 48?' (Winston knew that page 48 is where Napoleon's dogs chase Snowball into exile.)

'We shall see,' Winston said.

This produced a vast heaving of Snowball's fifteen stone and a long grunt of rage. The boy didn't fancy his chances in the confined space between the bales of straw.

'Page 48 was written by Dr O. and never happened,' he said hastily.

'Are you sure?'

'Quite sure, yes.'

'Thank you, comrade.'

Naturally Winston lost no time in reporting this conversation to Squealer – indeed Napoleon raised no objection to the boy's secret rendezvous with Snowball provided he always reported back.

[*NOTE. In Eric's manuscript the whole of this last sentence had been crossed out, but I could still read it.*]

Squealer once again proved his versatility. To a packed meeting in the barn he announced that Comrade Napoleon had solved the problem of 'we shall see' by means of 'scientific analysis' and 'new information'. Only the first 47 pages of the book were Mr B.'s and therefore true; everything that followed, or almost everything, belonged to Dr O. and was 'an imperialist human slander against animals everywhere'.

Squealer turned to Winston (perched in his usual position below the stage and to one side). 'Agreed, comrade?'

Winston nodded. Snowball's ears were twitching with suspicion.

'A nod is as good as a wink!' announced Benjamin, then resumed his steady chewing of hay.

Boxer and Clover took up the new chant: 'First 47 pages true!' The pigs, the sheep, the hens, the geese, and the cows all agreed that Napoleon was Absolutely Right about the first 47 pages and about everything. But Snowball was never quite reassured. As the dreaded page 48 approached, he tended to glance over his shoulder and cock his ear for the sound of dogs. It was probably no accident that page 48 occurred while Winston was in school. Snowball and his leading followers duly made their hasty exit through the fence, pursued by Napoleon's elite Dog Corps, trained in the loft above the harness room.

Once again all the animals were summoned to the barn. Squealer trotted about, marshalling the porkers, sows and piglets to fill the large gap on the platform left by the 'treacherous Snowballers'.

'New scientific analysis,' Squealer announced, 'reveals that the book was written by Mr B. up to page 48 – and no further.'

Squealer turned to Winston. The boy nodded, while chewing a cheese sandwich with pickle.

But a week later it was written on the barn door that the book had been right up to page 60. Winston found Boxer, Clover, Muriel, Benjamin and a crowd of sheep studying the words and arguing intently about what they meant. Boxer slowly ambled over and bent from his great height to nudge the boy's shoulder with his white-striped nose.

'How many pages are there after sixty?' he asked.

'Quite a few,' Winston said.

'Hm,' the old donkey Benjamin mused. 'Quite a few sounds quite a lot.'

From that time on this great survivor and wit took to asking, before bedding down for the night:

'Which page are we on, comrades?'

The weeks passed. Napoleon and his chosen acolytes among the pigs moved into the farmhouse, sleeping in the beds (but not with sheets, Squealer was at pains to let it be known), and dining off the Crown Derby china plate. Some hams found hanging in the kitchen were taken out for burial. Squealer announced that the Comrade Chairman, Helmsman and Leader (as Napoleon now styled himself, with medals to match) deserved the dignity and seclusion not to be obtained in a mere sty. Winston heard that Napoleon was sleeping in his parents' bed and Squealer in his own. Napoleon emerged from the house only rarely; and after a while he was almost never seen except on giant hoardings which the boy was instructed to commission in Porterstone. By chance, Knacker Simmonds's son Sid had a knack with a paintbrush and took on the commission with a chuckle, accepting as payment Winston's promise to deliver Boxer and Clover to him when their time came.

[*NOTE. This last sentence had also been crossed out by Eric.*]

One Sunday everyone was called to the yard. An enormous feast had been laid out (though most of it had been carefully set down on the platform reserved for the pigs). Napoleon finally arrived preceded by ten guard dogs and one of Sid's portraits [*deleted by Eric after 'dogs'*].

'Comrades!' shrieked Squealer. 'It is my revolutionary duty and honour to inform you that new scientific analysis has revealed the whole of *Animal Farm* to have been written by Mr B. in accordance with Scientific Animalism.'

As usual Squealer then scampered across in Winston's direction. The boy offered his normal nod.

'A nod is as good as a wink,' said Benjamin, adding: 'Comrades, we're no longer on any page. We have fallen off the book.'

'What is more,' Squealer went on in high excitement, 'Comrade Chairman Helmsman Leader Napoleon hereby announces a new tactical turn in our policy: the NEP!'

'NEP?' Benjamin asked loudly, relying on his clown's licence. 'You're sure it isn't NIP?'

One or two of the younger animals laughed. Clover hushed them.

'New Economic Policy, comrades,' Squealer explained. 'We are now into the managerial revolution. A managerial revolution requires a farm manager. Our great Leader in his wisdom has appointed that manager.'

Squealer paused dramatically. Every animal studied his neighbour and concluded that the new farm manager must be someone else. And then they were all looking at Winston because Squealer was looking at Winston.

Most of the animals were far from happy with this news. Snowball's distrust of humans had not been forgotten, particularly by the young, though his name could now be spoken only in whispers or, to be quite safe, not at all. Tolerating a single human 'guest' had been one thing – but a human farm manager was quite another. Of course Winston had been just that for quite a while in everything but name – but names are the most important commodity during revolutions. Even Boxer and Clover looked puzzled and uneasy. Their giant hoofs moved restlessly in the straw and a brood of little ducklings close by set up a commotion. Clover bent her misty eyes over them in consternation but they were all safe.

Winston was invited to tea in the farmhouse by 'his Excellency'. He forced himself to obey, though the filth and stink tore his heart. Dancing around Napoleon's chair, Squealer made a great thing about Winston's well-known liking for chocolate cake, which his Excellency had gone to enormous pains to 'procure' in his honour. The boy took one look at what was being offered, fought down his nausea, bit into it – and promptly spat it out.

To defend the 'conquests of Animalism' (Squealer was explaining) his Excellency had wisely been expanding his dog army by offering each breeding bitch additional bones and biscuits for each whelp. So well had this policy succeeded that his Excellency was now in a position to liberate several adjoining farms, or parts of farms, or overgrown bits and pieces neglected by Pilkington and Frederick. (The Great Patriotic War had unfortunately given way to the new Anti-Imperialist War through no fault of Napoleon's, who wanted only Peaceful Co-existence, Squealer explained.)

Napoleon's master plan was to establish a chain of Animal Democracies – to be known privately as satellites. Animal Farm's human neighbours were slow to react. Frederick and Pilkington were unable to join forces, being currently engaged in half a dozen lawsuits over boundaries, fences, water rights and dams. Napoleon's military campaign was a triumph and even his broad breast could no longer support the new medals he awarded himself; they began to spread down his shoulders to his thickening hams and rump. But it would be wrong to conclude that Animal Rule was extended effortlessly. Expanding beyond the fences and hedges of Animal Farm, Napoleon's praetorian guard of dogs and pigs frequently encountered animals who were in two minds about the blessings of the Great Pig's protection. Nothing excited Napoleon's fury and contempt like the pondering and dithering of the 'Two-Minders'. Indeed Squealer rapidly broadcast the slogan:

'Rout and trounce the Two-Minders!'

Only One-Minded animals, he explained, could triumph over One-Minded humans.

To Winston's surprise, and Squealer's fury, Boxer and Clover slowly shook their heads in stubborn disagreement.

'We're in two minds about that,' said the old stallion.

'Two minds may be twice as many as one mind,' Benjamin nodded, slowly stretching his spine with a prolonged yawn, then promptly falling asleep.

What had happened was this: Boxer and Clover had been despatched to haul heavy loads of grain and turnips to the new Animal Democracies (the loads were somehow always heavier on the return journey). Trundling between the farms,

Boxer had encountered animals brimming with strange news. Apparently the humans of England had recently elected a new type of government, a 'Labour Government', which was a great deal friendlier to toiling animals than Pilkington, Frederick and – the bolder spirits dared to add – Napoleon. Boxer heard that all farm land would soon be 'nationalised', like the coal mines and railways, with immense benefit to the animals. A new, 'progressive' type of human farm manager would put the welfare of animals above price and profit. According to rumour, the old slaughterhouses would be closed down. Knacker Simmonds and his son Sid were reported to be preparing for flight.

Boxer now related all this quite fearlessly, causing much whoofing, whinnying and lowing among the animals of Napoleon's domain. The old stallion's word was not to be doubted. Winston could see that Napoleon's acolytes were seething to set the dogs on Boxer. However, Boxer's hoof was a formidable weapon and his throat was a long way from the ground.

The pigs went into an agitated huddle in the farmhouse. Half an hour later Squealer bounced out into the yard where the animals had congregated.

'Comrades! Need I remind you of the wisdom of old Major? It was he who warned us that "Humans Will Always Be Humans".'

Consternation was written into Boxer's brow and his head dropped. He enormously admired old Major (who had been asleep for several months) and would do nothing to betray his teachings. It was the donkey Benjamin who broke the ensuing silence:

'Isn't Comrade Winston a human? I may be half blind but I've never seen him walk on four legs. I may be half deaf but I distinctly remember his appointment as our farm manager.'

'That's different!' snapped the enraged Squealer.

A few days later, Napoleon and Squealer suddenly agreed to elections in the new Animal Democracies. 'So what's new?' Squealer asked. Voting, he explained, is like signing your name: 'There are no two ways about it.'

The Two-Minders in the new Animal Democracies, however, were not easily swayed. They wanted the ballot papers to offer the following choices:

1. A Revolutionary Federation with Animal Farm.
2. An Appeal to the Labour Government.

Squealer was furious.

'We all know what this dirty game amounts to,' he pranced around the yard. 'It's not scientific, comrades, it's not dialectical, it's not deterministic.' He turned sharply: 'Isn't that the case, Comrade Winston?'

The boy nodded with more conviction than usual. He wasn't much interested in politics, but his father and all the other adults of Porterstone had always said that 'nationalisation' of the land would be nothing short of daylight robbery. By now he regarded Animal Rule as a sad absurdity, an affront to the natural order of things and doomed to failure – whereas 'nationalisation' of the farms would be a permanent catastrophe.

As Commissar for Elections, Squealer then read out the single question which Comrade Napoleon in his infinite wisdom had decreed should be written on the ballot paper:

'Do I vote to liberate myself from the cruelty and ritual slaughter of the human oppressors by merging my destiny with the brave comrades of Animal Farm under the wise and benevolent guidance of Comrade Chairman Napoleon, Peace Be With Him?'

Shortly before the elections were held a large number of notorious Two-Minders living in the new Animal Democracies mysteriously disappeared from their stalls, poops, kennels and nests. They vanished. But there was no blood, no gore, no ripped-out feathers, nothing to disturb the other animals. Benjamin suggested to Boxer that there might be a human hand in all this, and Boxer sadly reflected that Winston had not been seen much lately.

After a suitable interval Squealer began pinning to doors and trees the Collective Confession of the Two-Minders:

'Two-Mindism is a human conspiracy,' they admitted. 'Pilkington and Frederick put us up to it. Comrade Napoleon has been right all along. Rout and trounce the Two-Minders! We demand our own punishment.'

But Napoleon in his great mercy decreed clemency. All parties had now agreed to settle their 'comradely differences' under the new One-Mind Animal Front, which would sponsor the single question on the ballot paper. By way of celebration, extra rations of milk and mash were provided. The warrior dogs were feasted on hare and rabbit (who weren't entitled to vote). The election was a great success. Those voting 'Yes' were instructed to place their ballot papers in large milk churns; those voting 'No' were told to deposit theirs in a crow's nest high in the sycamore tree. Ladders were provided by Winston, on written request and payment of a deposit.

Squealer announced that 99.99 per cent of the voters had said 'Yes' to Napoleon's question. He did not mention what proportion of animals had actually voted.

After the triumphant elections, all of the Animal Democracies banned Two-Mindism and hailed Napoleon as their

Genius. His Seventh Birthday was officially celebrated as his Seventieth. There was quite a hullabaloo and a definite upsurge in the Cult of the Pig. Napoleon and his closest collaborators locked themselves into the farmhouse for eighty-four hours, slurping beer from the barrel. By the second night of the party Napoleon was to be heard bellowing and roaring words previously unheard:

'Pigthink! Pigspeak! Pigsoc! Pigcrime!'

Napoleon issued orders that an Iron Fence was to be erected round the farm. All other labour was to cease until the Fence had been completed under Winston's supervision. A week after Napoleon's birthday all the creatures on the farm were divided by decree into three categories: the Inner Party, the Outer Party, and the Proles.

Only pigs were eligible for the Inner Party. Toiling at the Iron Fence, sweat running down his withered shanks, Boxer told Winston how proud he was that he, Clover and Benjamin had been assigned to the Outer Party in recognition of 'revolutionary service beyond the call of duty'.

Some time after Napoleon and Squealer declared *Animal Farm* to be one hundred per cent in accordance with Scientific Animalism, the book was one hundred per cent banned.

Winston was ordered to build a bonfire in the yard for the ceremonial book-burning. Only he could create fire. But the boy felt a deep, natural stirring in his gut against this tyranny. His decent instincts demanded resistance. He therefore decided [*deleted*] As the last man on the farm he

[*Eric's new fairy story ended abruptly, in mid-sentence. Below the last line he had scribbled a few words:*

'This was to have been the first chapter of a sequel to Animal Farm *but it has turned out rather too reactionary for my taste and I'm*

tempted to abandon my ill-fated animals. Of course people will get the wrong end of the stick whatever one writes.']

The events described in *Dr Orwell and Mr Blair* are entirely fictitious. None of it ever happened.

GARAGE

H & H Zweite Hand Kleidermarkt GmbH
Ahornstr. 2
10878 Berlin
Phone 030 21 12 760

Blouse à DM 26,00
#2000 26,00 A

Summe 26,00 *
Gegeben 50,00
Wechselgeld 24,00

Bar

A) 16,00% MwSt = 3,59 DM

Vielen Dank für Ihren Einkauf!

Second Hand Ware ist leider vom Umtausch ausgeschlossen. Bitte besuchen Sie auch unsere Filialen "Made in Berlin" - Potsdamer Str. 106 10785 Berlin und "Colours" - Bergmannstr. 102 10961 Berlin.

Thank you for shopping with us!

Sorry - no refund, nor exchange or credit on merchandise. Please come again!

13:26 011 00031 100

GARAGE
N + H Zweite Hand Kleidermarkt GmbH
Ahornstr. 2
10878 Berlin
Phone 030 21 12 760

Kiloware à DM 25,00

#2000	26,00 a

Summe	26,00 *
Gegeben	50,00
Wechselgeld	24,00
	========

Bar

A) 16,00% MwSt = 3,59 DM

Vielen Dank für Ihren Einkauf!

Second Hand Ware ist leider vom Umtausch ausgeschlossen. Bitte besuchen Sie auch unsere Filialen "Made in Berlin" - Potsdamer Str. 106 - 10785 Berlin und "Colours" - Bergmannstr. 102 - 10961 Berlin.

Thank you for shopping with us!

Sorry - no refund, nor exchange or credit on merchandise. Please come again!

[illegible]7.98 15:26 011 00054 100